The Story World

The Story World

RUTH TOOZE, *Editor*
> *Specialist in children's literature*
> *Author of* Literature and Music *and* Your Children Want to Read

ANNE NEIGOFF, *Managing Editor*

Special Advisory Committee:

Mary E. Ferguson, *Elementary Supervisor*
> Atlantic City Public Schools, Atlantic City, New Jersey

Julia Weber Gordon, *Director of the Office of Child and Youth Study*
> New Jersey State Department of Education

Anne S. Hoppock, *Director of Elementary Education*
> New Jersey State Department of Education

The CHILD'S WORLD inc. | Chicago | 1968

Acknowledgments

THE EDITORS AND PUBLISHERS wish to thank the following publishers, authors, and agents whose permission to use and reprint stories, poems, and illustrations has made this book possible:

ABELARD-SCHUMAN LIMITED
for "Wise," from *Runny Days, Sunny Days* by Aileen Fisher, copyright 1958 by Aileen Fisher.

THOMAS Y. CROWELL COMPANY
for "Jareb and the Contest" from *Jareb* by Miriam Powell, copyright 1952 by Miriam Powell.

DOUBLEDAY & COMPANY
for "Robin Saves the Day" from *The Door in the Wall* by Marguerite de Angeli, copyright 1949 by Marguerite de Angeli.

DOUBLEDAY & COMPANY and
CURTIS BROWN, LTD.
for "Navaho Friend" from *Navaho Sister* by Evelyn Sibley Lampman, copyright 1956 by Evelyn Sibley Lampman.

CAROLYN W. DRISCOLL
for "Hold Fast Your Dreams" by Louise Driscoll.

HARCOURT, BRACE & COMPANY, INC.
for "The Missing Dollar" from *Across the Bridge* by Jerrold Beim, copyright 1951 by Jerrold Beim; "The Little Foxes" from *Miracles on Maple Hill* by Virginia Sorensen, copyright 1956 by Virginia Sorensen; "Share and Share Alike" from *The Moffats* by Eleanor Estes, copyright 1941 by Eleanor Estes.

HARPER & BROTHERS
for "Maggie Rose's Christmas Birthday" from *Maggie Rose* by Ruth Sawyer, copyright 1952 by Ruth Sawyer Durand; "Andre" from *Bronzeville Boys and Girls* by Gwendolyn Brooks, copyright 1956 by Gwendolyn Brooks Blakely; "Old Log House" from *A World to Know* by James S. Tippett, copyright 1933 by Harper & Brothers.

HARPER & BROTHERS and
METHUEN & COMPANY, LTD., LONDON
for "Dance at Grandpa's" from *Little House in the Big Woods* by Laura Ingalls Wilder, copyright 1932 by Laura Ingalls Wilder. Illustrations by Garth Williams, copyright 1953 by Garth Williams.

HOUGHTON MIFFLIN COMPANY
for "The Sun" from *All About Me* by John Drinkwater.

J. B. LIPPINCOTT COMPANY and
ANN WATKINS, INC.
for "There Isn't Time" from *Over the Garden Wall* by Eleanor Farjeon, copyright 1933, 1951 by Eleanor Farjeon.

McGRAW-HILL BOOK COMPANY, INC.
for "The Pony Race" from *Windy Foot at the County Fair* by Frances Frost, published by Whittlesey House, copyright 1947 by the McGraw-Hill Book Company, Inc.; "A Penny's Worth of Character" from *A Penny's Worth of Character* by Jesse Stuart, copyright 1954 by Jesse Stuart and Robert Henneberger.

THE MACMILLAN COMPANY
for "My Gift" from *Sing Song* by Christina Rossetti; "Barter" from *Collected Poems* by Sara Teasdale.

THE MACMILLAN COMPANY, THE SOCIETY OF AUTHORS, and DR. JOHN MASEFIELD, O.M.
for "Sea Fever" from *Collected Poems* by John Masefield.

G. P. PUTNAM'S SONS
for *A Cheese for Lafayette* by Elisabeth Meg, copyright 1950 by Elizabeth Wenning Goepp and Margaret Webb Sanders.

THE SOCIETY OF AUTHORS
for "The Horseman" from *Rhymes and Verses* by Walter de la Mare, permission of the Literary Trustees of Walter de la Mare and The Society of Authors as their representative.

THE VIKING PRESS, INC.
for "The Blue Willow Plate" from *Blue Willow* by Doris Gates, copyright 1940 by Doris Gates; "The Wooden Locket" from *The Wooden Locket* by Alice Alison Lide and Margaret Alison Johansen, copyright 1953 by Alice Alison Lide and Margaret Alison Johansen.

HENRY Z. WALCK, INC.
for "The Stock Show" from *Lucky Mischief* by Mebane Holoman Burgwyn, copyright 1949 by Henry Z. Walck, Inc.

Care has been taken to obtain permission to use copyright material. Any errors are unintentional and will be corrected in future printings if notice is sent to CHILD'S WORLD, INC.

Every day is an adventure, and adventure is everywhere. Today we can fly a plane around the world or send a rocket into space — but we can find adventure, too, in our own home and school. For wherever there are people, there are exciting things, funny things, puzzling things happening.

Do you know why? It is because every person in the world is different —and yet all people are alike in many ways. Getting to know the new boy or girl across the street can be an adventure. Getting to know a boy from Japan or a girl from France can be an adventure, too. Can you guess another way people have always liked to go adventuring? It is in the pages of a book.

Stories can take you forward or backward in time. In them, you can meet new friends from many lands around the world. Some will make you feel at home at once. Others may seem a little strange at first, but as you step into their lives and share their laughter and their doubts, you will find that they are not so very different after all.

The things that happened to them may have happened to you, too— although perhaps not exactly in the same way. In this book, you will find a story of a boy who had to bring help to a besieged castle. You never had to do this—but you have met fear in other ways and had to face it bravely. Like the boys and girls in these stories, you have been happy or lonely, have won a race or lost it, have wondered and asked why and found that not all problems are in an arithmetic book. Sometimes even your best friend can be a problem!

We hope that as you read these stories, you will find that they help you understand more about yourself and your world, for all boys and girls everywhere share the greatest adventure of all—the adventure of growing up.

Table of Contents

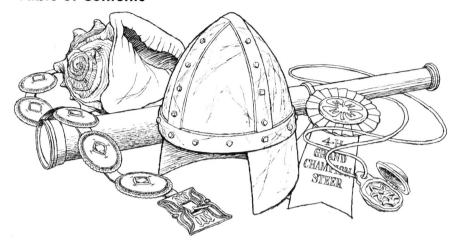

The Pony Race

BY FRANCES FROST

Illustrated by Wesley Dennis

The County Fair was fun for Toby, Betsy, young Johnny, and their father and mother—the Clark family. They rode the Ferris Wheel, watched the fireworks, and entered contests and exhibits. Best of all, Toby discovered new friends in Tish Burnham, a girl who was different, and in the jockey, Billy Blue. He found new courage, too, to fight the bully, Lem Strout, even though it cost him two black eyes. Then came the exciting day when Toby rode his pony, Windy Foot, in the Pony Race.

AT HALF-PAST ONE, Toby hurried up the road toward Burnham's stable. He was wearing his light-blue slacks and shirt that he had been saving for the race, and his old sneakers that he had ridden Windy Foot in, all summer. The wind was warm, but he shivered.

He began to run. At the stable, Billy Blue was standing in the yard, his old pipe puffing like a stub chimney in his mouth and his safety pins gleaming on his pants leg.

"Kittens!" said Billy Blue, giving him an over-all survey. "I guessed right on my color scheme. Come on in, Toby."

Windy Foot was as clean as a whistle. His hoofs were polished. His dappled hide was spotless. And his heavy black mane and his heavy black tail were braided with narrow blue-and-white ribbons so that he looked like a pony out of a fairy tale. His forelock was tied up in a splash of ribbons and his tail was a wonder of blue and white fancy braiding. The black saddle and the black bridle had been rubbed until they held the deep gleam of excellent leather.

Toby couldn't believe his eyes. "Barnacles!" he said in a whisper.

"Barnacles, nothing," said Billy Blue. "Now you and Windy match by way of decoration, and the saddle matches those shiners you're wearing. You'd better get down to the gate and check in. The race starts at two-thirty."

"Yes, sir," answered Toby, still gazing at Windy Foot. "Mr. Blue, did you wind up Windy like this yourself?"

Billy Blue choked on his pipe smoke. "Got to do something to waste my time. Back him out! How do you think he's going to run a race standing in a stall?"

"Thanks, Mr. Blue!"

"Pshaw," said Billy Blue, looking out of the stable door.

Toby put his cheek against Windy's. "All right, boy, here we go!"

He backed the pony out of the stall, into the yard, and mounted him. "Thanks again, Mr. Blue." His voice croaked. Windy looked so beautiful that it made his throat ache.

"Oh, *cats!*" said Billy Blue loudly. "Stop talking and ride!"

At the checking place in the trampled field outside the track gate, Toby dismounted and held Windy's bridle, waiting his turn. His heart was acting like a hoptoad in his chest.

Ahead of him was the tow-headed boy he had seen exercising a brown pony. The boy wore tan shorts and a tan sport shirt; his hair gleamed almost white in the sunlight; and his pony wore a big yellow ribbon on her mane and another on her tail. The checker was gazing sternly at the boy's entry ticket. He nodded, filed it in a tin box, stood up and took an arm band from a pile on his table.

"All right, Jones. Stand still." With a safety pin, the man fastened the top of the white canvas band to Jones' left shoulder, then tied the bottom of the band around his arm with tapes. The large, black numeral on the band read 2. "That means you're in number two position from the inside rail," he explained. "You wait up the field there, where the Burnham girl is."

"Thank you," said Jones faintly and led his pony off.

Toby had a bad moment when he thought he had lost his entry ticket. The man watched while he dug in his pockets. He found it in his back pocket finally, tucked among the pages of his sketch pad.

"Whew!" he breathed thankfully and handed it to the checker.

"O. K., Clark," the man said and started to fasten an arm band on him. Then his hands dropped from Toby's shoulder. "Looks as if you've been in a little scrap. Can you see all right?" The man peered at him.

"Yes, sir," Toby gulped. "I can see!"

"How about that left eye?" asked the man severely.

"It's all right today." What if the man wouldn't let him ride? Toby's stomach hit his sneakers. "I can see first rate," he told the checker earnestly. "It just looks black."

"Black? Purple, you mean." The man hesitated for a moment. "Well, all right. I'll take your word for it." He finished fastening the arm band. "That must have been some fight." He smiled slightly. "Number three position from the inside rail."

"Oh, thanks!" Toby sighed with relief. He led Windy down the field as Lem Strout rode up to the checking point. Toby's heart did a back flip. Lem would be fourth, right next to him. He told himself fiercely that he wasn't afraid of Lem any more, and walked up to Tish and Jones.

11

"Hello, Toby." Tish wore white duck pants and a white linen shirt and had a white ribbon in her dark hair. Her arm band said 1. "How do you feel?"

She looked wonderful, he thought. He still wished he could do a portrait sketch of her. "Funny," he answered. "How do you?"

"Oh, fine," she said, smiling at him. "You won't feel funny when you get started."

He was skeptical. He patted Jigs. The heavy-footed black pony had green and gold ribbons wound in her mane and tail. "Did Billy Blue decorate Jigs, too?"

Tish looked at Windy. "He loves doing it. He's decorated my ponies every year. He had a boy of his own once who died when he was ten, and I guess Billy's thinking of him when he buys ribbons and does all the braiding. Toby, do you know Dicky Jones? Dicky, this is Toby Clark."

Dicky's jutting jaw seemed more prominent than ever, but his blue eyes were frightened. "Hello," he murmured.

"Hello, Jones," said Toby and held out his hand. "This your first race?" He felt as scared as Jones looked, but he was older and couldn't show it. Well, maybe it would help Jones if he knew somebody else was scared, as well as he.

Jones nodded.

"Mine, too. I'm scared."

Jones' eyes lost some of their fright. "Are you? So am I."

Tish patted Jigs' side, not looking at the boys. "What are you scared about? All you have to do is ride."

Toby and Jones laughed nervously.

"Here comes Lem," said Tish.

Lem wore overalls, and his sorrel pony had pink and black ribbons twisted in his mane like the pink and black strips wound on the handles of the ten-cent whips in the whip-and-balloon stand. He gave Toby a baleful glare and led the sorrel away from the group.

"Oh, I forgot to tell you," said Tish, "your father invited Jerry and me down to your farm for Christmas, and Jerry said Yes."

"He did? Hooray!" Toby began to plan all the things they would do at Christmas—coasting and skiing and skating on Crooked River and popping corn and—

"Look at Jimmy!" said Tish.

Deep in thought, Jimmy came toward them with his head down. Tucked into his washed dungarees was a red-and-white plaid flannel shirt open at the throat. The pinto, Whistle Stop, wore simply a red-and-white saddle blanket.

"My gosh!" exclaimed Toby. "Where's his saddle?"

"He never uses one in a race. Didn't I tell you? Jimmy, wake up!" Tish was laughing.

Jimmy lifted his head in surprise. "Oh, hello." He nodded vaguely. "Isn't it nearly time to start?"

"Nearly," answered Tish. She didn't smile. "Jimmy. What are you worrying about?"

"Tractor," he answered briefly. "Oh, Toby. Hi."

"Hi," said Toby.

Here was Jimmy worrying about winning the race so he could put ten dollars toward his father's tractor, here was Tish wanting to put ten dollars toward medical college, here was Jones, wanting to win so he could—what? Toby didn't know what Jones wanted. And there was Lem Strout, wanting to win the race so he could help *his* father, probably. Well, but Dad and Windy Foot—

Jimmy interrupted his thinking. "Toby, your father spoke to my father this morning about Christmas. We'd like to, but we can't get down. We always have a lot of work planned to do during Christmas vacation—mending harness and carpenter work around the place. Thanks for asking us, though."

"I wish you could come, Jimmy."

"Here's the roan!" said Tish. "It's time!"

Toby quivered. He stroked Windy Foot's nose. "Here we go, boy," he murmured. Windy looked at him and shook his blue-and-white plaited mane. Toby mounted him and laid an unsteady hand on the dappled neck. Windy whinnied. He wanted to start running. Toby held him in. "Easy, Windy, easy," he said and tried to stop trembling.

The young woman in the scarlet coat and the black derby hat rode up to the ponies. "All ready?" she asked with a smile.

"I guess we're all ready," Tish said, glancing around.

13

"I'll lead you up to the quarter-mile post," explained the young woman. "Get into position according to your numbers, starting with number one at the inside rail. When you have passed the finish post, all ponies return and line up in front of the judges' stand."

She turned the roan and Tish followed her. Dicky Jones rode after Tish. Toby walked Windy behind Jones, acutely conscious of Lem behind him on the sorrel. Jimmy and the pinto tagged the procession. The band was playing a loud, gay march and the trumpets flashed in the sun.

Toby bit his lips. He guessed he was more scared than Jones. His heart was thumping like a bass drum. He wanted to look at the grandstand and see if he could locate the family, but he knew it would be useless. Instead, he watched the young woman on the Kentucky roan and took his place at the starting post beside Jones. Jones was very pale. The poor kid, Toby thought.

He couldn't resist glancing at Lem. Lem was jerking at the sorrel's

bit and muttering under his breath. Toby caught Jimmy's eye. Jimmy winked, then settled himself on Whistle Stop's red-and-white blanket. Toby tried to wink back and his shiners shut up. He opened them quickly again.

The roan pranced off around the track and out of the gate. The starter held a watch and a whistle. He was a stout red-faced man and he kept mopping his forehead with a blue bandanna. The band stopped playing with a flourish of drums. Toby's blood was roaring in his ears. The starter's whistle shrilled sharply. Toby gulped. Windy Foot shot forward.

The ponies ran together for a breath. Toby leaned forward on Windy's neck. "Excuse my dust!" he shouted.

For some crazy reason he wasn't scared now. He felt Windy gather speed and he gathered all of himself together and rode. A vast joy surged through him. He and Windy Foot had one heart and one mind.

He left Jones behind. The brown pony was slow. Then he was a neck ahead of Tish. Jimmy, crouched like an Indian on the pinto, was a shoulder's length ahead of Windy. But Lem was yelling beside him, coming closer to Windy, crowding him.

"Sissy!" screamed Lem.

Toby thought fast. If Lem pushed him over, he'd have to run into Tish and they'd both tangle with the fence, and Tish would be hurt. Clean rage swept him. They were nearing the turn.

"Tish!" he shouted at the top of his lungs. "Get ahead!" He pulled on Windy's reins, holding him up, falling behind, and Tish pounded past, rounding the turn. Then just as Lem was about to shove him into the fence, Toby yelled in Windy's ear, "Dust, Windy!" and pulled to the right.

Windy spurted forward, his hind quarters barely missing the nose of Lem's pony, and there was a crash behind him. A cry went up from the grandstand, but he couldn't look back. They were around the turn. Jigs began to lag, but Jimmy and Whistle Stop were streaking for the finish post.

Toby begged, "Dust, Windy!"

Windy dusted, and as they neared the finish post, Windy and Whistle Stop were nose and nose.

"Oh, dust!" Toby sobbed.

Windy flew past the post half a neck ahead of Whistle Stop.

Toby was panting and drenched with sweat. As he pulled his heaving pony up, he discovered that he was crying. He sniffled, heard Jimmy whistle to the pinto, and saw Whistle Stop come to a halt. He turned Windy, rubbed his arm across his wet face, and rode back, side by side with Jimmy, too breathless to speak. Tish and Jones followed. The grandstand was ominously silent.

Then Jimmy said, his voice hoarse with anger, "I saw what Lem tried to do. Look, Toby! He hit the fence himself."

Toby looked. Lem's sorrel lay kicking at the fence. Lem was limping down the track toward the outside fence.

Toby put his hand on Windy's sweaty neck. Jimmy gently twisted Whistle Stop's mane. Tish leaned over Jigs' black neck and said something quietly to her. Jones patted the rump of his brown pony.

Toby guessed they were all thinking the same thing: it might have been Windy Foot or Jigs or Whistle or the brown pony that was hurt.

Jimmy said quietly, "That'll disqualify Lem for next year."

"I guess he won't bother anyone in a race again," added Tish.

When the track was clear, one of the judges came down from the stand. Another, with a megaphone, announced loudly, "Ladies and gentlemen, we regret that this accident has delayed the awarding of the prize for the annual Webster County Fair Pony Race for ponies three years old or under. Will the owners of the ponies please dismount?" He waited until they were standing on the ground. "The prize of ten dollars for first place in the race goes this year to entry Number 3—Windy Foot, three-year-old Shetland, ridden by Tobias Clark, the young man with the shiners!"

Toby felt his face grow hot and his stomach did handsprings. He thought of Jimmy's tractor and of Tish's medical college. Then he thought of Dad's corn-cutter blade and the leaky milkhouse. The grandstand shouted and clapped.

The judge not in the stand walked up to Toby, said, "Good riding, Clark," and handed him an envelope. He shook hands, patted Windy, and returned to the stand.

17

Toby stared at the envelope.

Jimmy grinned at him. "What're you looking so glum about? It was a swell race!"

Tish smiled and her eyes were glowing. "Hooray for Windy!"

Toby began to feel better. "Come on, let's go," he said. "We're holding up the Fair."

Jones said timidly, "Congratulations!"

"Thanks, Jones," said Toby.

They led the ponies to the gate while the band played a lilting tune. Toby's heart lilted, too.

Well, he thought, the race was over, the Fair was over for him, and it had been wonderful. He had learned a great deal about people, and he had made four good friends—Tish and Jimmy and Mr. Burnham and Billie Blue. And he could even feel sorry for Lem. He put a finger on his left eye shiner. It was still pretty sore, but anyway he was glad he'd have some decorations to show Cliff when he got home. He could look forward to Christmas when Tish and her father would be visiting them. And next year he would enter some drawings of horses at the Fair's art exhibition.

He remembered the Roman candle feeling he'd had in his chest at the beginning of the Fair. But now, thinking of home, he felt as if he had a good warm sun glowing steadily where his heart should be.

Dance at Grandpa's

BY LAURA INGALLS WILDER

Illustrated by Garth Williams

Long ago, in 1872, there was a Little House on the edge
of the Big Woods of Wisconsin. In it lived Ma and
Pa Ingalls and Laura and Mary and Baby Carrie. They
were far away from any settlement, and they had no
near neighbors. Laura and Mary helped with the
work and shared the family adventures and hardships of
those pioneer days. But there were love and laughter, too,
and gay, good times as you will read in this story of what
happened at the Dance at Grandpa's.

MONDAY MORNING everybody got up early, in a hurry to get
started to Grandpa's. Pa wanted to be there to help with the work of
gathering and boiling the sap. Ma would help Grandma and the aunts
make good things to eat for all the people who were coming to the
dance.

Breakfast was eaten and the dishes washed and the beds made by
lamplight. Pa packed his fiddle carefully in its box and put it in the
big sled that was already waiting at the gate.

The air was cold and frosty and the light was gray, when Laura
and Mary and Ma with Baby Carrie were tucked in snug and warm
under the robes on the straw in the bottom of the sled.

The horses shook their heads and pranced, making the sleigh bells
ring merrily, and away they went on the road through the Big Woods
to Grandpa's.

The snow was damp and smooth in the road, so the sled slipped quickly over it, and the big trees seemed to be hurrying by on either side.

After awhile there was sunshine in the woods and the air sparkled. The long streaks of yellow light lay between the shadows of the tree trunks, and the snow was colored faintly pink. All the shadows were thin and blue and every little curve of snowdrifts and every little track in the snow had a shadow.

Pa showed Laura the tracks of the wild creatures in the snow at the sides of the road. The small, leaping tracks of cottontail rabbits, the tiny tracks of field mice, and the feather-stitching tracks of snowbirds. There were larger tracks, like dogs' tracks, where foxes had run, and there were the tracks of a deer that had bounded away into the woods.

The air was growing warmer already and Pa said that the snow wouldn't last long.

It did not seem long until they were sweeping into the clearing at Grandpa's house, all the sleigh bells jingling. Grandma came to the door and stood there smiling, calling to them to come in.

She said that Grandpa and Uncle George were already at work out in the maple woods. So Pa went to help them, while Laura and Mary and Ma, with Baby Carrie in her arms, went into Grandma's house and took off their wraps.

Laura loved Grandma's house. It was much larger than their house at home. There was one great big room, and then there was a little room that belonged to Uncle George, and there was another room for the aunts, Aunt Docia and Aunt Ruby. And then there was the kitchen, with a big cookstove.

It was fun to run the whole length of the big room, from the large fireplace at one end all the way to Grandma's bed, under the window in the other end. The floor was made of wide thick slabs that Grandpa had hewed from the logs with his ax. The floor was smoothed all over, and scrubbed clean and white, and the big bed under the window was soft with feathers.

The day seemed very short while Laura and Mary played in the big room and Ma helped Grandma and the aunts in the kitchen. The men

had taken their dinners to the maple woods, so for dinner they did not set the table, but ate cold venison sandwiches and drank milk. But for supper Grandma made hasty pudding.

She stood by the stove, sifting the yellow corn meal from her fingers into a kettle of boiling, salted water. She stirred the water all the time with a big wooden spoon, and sifted in the meal until the kettle was full of a thick, yellow, bubbling mass. Then she set it on the back of the stove where it would cook slowly.

It smelled good. The whole house smelled good, with the sweet and spicy smells from the kitchen, and the smell of the hickory logs burning with clear, bright flames in the fireplace, and the smell of a clove-apple beside Grandma's mending basket on the table. The sunshine came in through the sparkling window panes, and everything was large and spacious and clean.

At supper time Pa and Grandpa came from the woods. Each had on his shoulders a wooden yoke that Grandpa had made. It was cut to fit around their necks in the back, and hollowed out to fit over their shoulders. From each end hung a chain with a hook, and on each hook hung a big wooden bucket full of hot maple syrup.

Pa and Grandpa had brought the syrup from the big kettle in the woods. They steadied the buckets with their hands, but the weight hung from the yokes on their shoulders.

21

Grandma made room for a huge brass kettle on the stove. Pa and Grandpa poured the syrup into the brass kettle, and it was so large that it held all the syrup from the four big buckets.

Then Uncle George came with a smaller bucket of syrup, and everybody ate the hot hasty pudding with maple syrup for supper.

Uncle George was home from the army. He wore his blue army coat with the brass buttons, and he had bold, merry blue eyes. He was big and broad and he walked with a swagger.

Laura looked at him all the time she was eating her hasty pudding, because she had heard Pa say to Ma that he was wild.

"George is wild, since he came back from the war," Pa had said, shaking his head as if he were sorry, but it couldn't be helped. Uncle George had run away to be a drummer boy in the army, when he was fourteen years old.

Laura had never seen a wild man before. She did not know whether she was afraid of Uncle George or not.

When supper was over, Uncle George went outside the door and blew his army bugle, long and loud. It made a lovely, ringing sound, far away through the Big Woods. The woods were dark and silent and the trees stood still as though they were listening. Then from very far away the sound came back, thin and clear and small, like a little bugle answering the big one.

"Listen," Uncle George said, "isn't that pretty?" Laura looked at him but she did not say anything, and when Uncle George stopped blowing the bugle she ran into the house.

Ma and Grandma cleared away the dishes and washed them, and swept the hearth, while Aunt Docia and Aunt Ruby made themselves pretty in their room.

Laura sat on their bed and watched them comb out their long hair and part it carefully. They parted it from their foreheads to the napes of their necks and then they parted it from ear to ear. They braided their back hair in long braids and then did the braids up carefully in big knots.

They had washed their hands and faces and scrubbed them well with soap, at the wash-basin on the bench in the kitchen. They had used store soap, not the slimy, soft, dark brown soap that Grandma made and kept in a big jar to use for common every day.

They fussed for a long time with their front hair, holding up the lamp and looking at their hair in the little looking-glass that hung on the log wall. They brushed it so smooth on each side of the straight white part that it shone like silk in the lamplight. The little puff on each side shone, too, and the ends were coiled and twisted neatly under the big knot in the back.

Then they pulled on their beautiful white stockings, that they had

knit of fine cotton thread in lacy, openwork patterns, and they buttoned up their best shoes. They helped each other with their corsets. Aunt Docia pulled as hard as she could on Aunt Ruby's corset strings, and then Aunt Docia hung on to the foot of the bed while Aunt Ruby pulled on hers.

"Pull, Ruby, pull!" Aunt Docia said, breathless. "Pull harder." So Aunt Ruby braced her feet and pulled harder. Aunt Docia kept measuring her waist with her hands, and at last she gasped, "I guess that's the best you can do."

She said, "Caroline says Charles could span her waist with his hands, when they were married."

Caroline was Laura's Ma, and when she heard this Laura felt proud.

Then Aunt Ruby and Aunt Docia put on their flannel petticoats and their plain petticoats and their stiff, starched white petticoats with knitted lace all around the flounces. And they put on their beautiful dresses.

Aunt Docia's dress was a sprigged print, dark blue, with sprigs of red flowers and green leaves thick upon it. The basque was buttoned down the front with black buttons which looked so exactly like juicy big blackberries that Laura wanted to taste them.

Aunt Ruby's dress was wine-colored calico, covered all over with a feathery pattern in lighter wine color. It buttoned with gold-colored buttons, and every button had a little castle and a tree carved on it.

Aunt Docia's pretty white collar was fastened in front with a large round cameo pin, which had a lady's head on it. But Aunt Ruby pinned her collar with a red rose made of sealing wax. She had made it herself, on the head of a darning needle which had a broken eye, so it couldn't be used as a needle any more.

They looked lovely, sailing over the floor so smoothly with their large round skirts. Their little waists rose up tight and slender in the middle, and their cheeks were red and their eyes bright, under the wings of shining, sleek hair.

Ma was beautiful, too, in her dark green delaine, with the little leaves that looked like strawberries scattered over it. The skirt was ruffled and flounced and draped and trimmed with knots of dark green

ribbon, and nestling at her throat was a gold pin. The pin was flat, as long and as wide as Laura's two biggest fingers, and it was carved all over, and scalloped on the edges. Ma looked so rich and fine that Laura was afraid to touch her.

People had begun to come. They were coming on foot through the snowy woods, with their lanterns, and they were driving up to the door in sleds and wagons. Sleigh bells were jingling all the time.

The big room filled with tall boots and swishing skirts, and ever so many babies were lying in rows on Grandma's bed. Uncle James and Aunt Libby had come with their little girl, whose name was Laura Ingalls, too. The two Lauras leaned on the bed and looked at the babies, and the other Laura said her baby was prettier than Baby Carrie.

25

"She is not, either!" Laura said. "Carrie's the prettiest baby in the whole world."

"No, she isn't," the other Laura said.

"Yes, she is!"

"No, she isn't!"

Ma came sailing over in her fine delaine, and said severely: "Laura!"

So neither Laura said anything more.

Uncle George was blowing his bugle. It made a loud, ringing sound in the big room, and Uncle George joked and laughed and danced, blowing the bugle. Then Pa took his fiddle out of its box and began to play, and all the couples stood in squares on the floor and began to dance when Pa called the figures.

"Grand right and left!" Pa called out, and all the skirts began to swirl and all the boots began to stamp. The circles went round and round, all the skirts going one way and all the boots going the other

way, and hands clasping and parting high up in the air.

"Swing your partners!" Pa called, and "Each gent bow to the lady on the left!"

They all did as Pa said. Laura watched Ma's skirt swaying and her little waist bending and her dark head bowing, and she thought Ma was the loveliest dancer in the world. The fiddle was singing:

"Oh, you Buffalo gals,
Aren't you coming out tonight,
Aren't you coming out tonight,
Aren't you coming out tonight,
Oh, you Buffalo gals,
Aren't you coming out tonight,
To dance by the light of the moon?"

The little circles and the big circles went round and round, and the skirts swirled and the boots stamped, and partners bowed and separated and met and bowed again.

27

In the kitchen Grandma was all by herself, stirring the boiling syrup in the big brass kettle. She stirred in time to the music. By the back door was a pail of clean snow, and sometimes Grandma took a spoonful of syrup from the kettle and poured it on some of the snow in a saucer.

Laura watched the dancers again. Pa was playing "The Irish Washerwoman" now. He called:

"Doe see, ladies, doe see doe,
Come down heavy on your heel and toe!"

Laura could not keep her feet still. Uncle George looked at her and laughed. Then he caught her by the hand and did a little dance with her, in the corner. She liked Uncle George.

Everybody was laughing, over by the kitchen door. They were dragging Grandma in from the kitchen. Grandma's dress was beautiful, too; a dark blue calico with autumn-colored leaves scattered over it. Her cheeks were pink from laughing, and she was shaking her head. The wooden spoon was in her hand.

"I can't leave the syrup," she said.

But Pa began to play "The Arkansas Traveler," and everybody began to clap in time to the music. So Grandma bowed to them all and did a few steps by herself. She could dance as prettily as any of them. The clapping almost drowned the music of Pa's fiddle.

Suddenly Uncle George did a pigeon wing, and bowing low before Grandma he began to jig. Grandma tossed her spoon to somebody. She put her hands on her hips and faced Uncle George, and everybody shouted. Grandma was jigging.

Laura clapped her hands in time to the music, with all the other clapping hands. The fiddle sang as it had never sung before. Grandma's eyes were snapping and her cheeks were red, and underneath her skirts her heels were clicking as fast as the thumping of Uncle George's boots.

Everybody was excited. Uncle George kept on jigging and Grandma kept on facing him, jigging too. The fiddle did not stop. Uncle George began to breathe loudly, and he wiped sweat off his forehead. Grandma's eyes twinkled.

"You can't beat her, George!" somebody shouted.

Uncle George jigged faster. He jigged twice as fast as he had been jigging. So did Grandma. Everybody cheered again. All the women were laughing and clapping their hands, and all the men were teasing George. George did not care, but he did not have breath enough to laugh. He was jigging.

Pa's blue eyes were snapping and sparking. He was standing up, watching George and Grandma, and the bow danced over the fiddle strings. Laura jumped up and down and squealed and clapped her hands.

Grandma kept on jigging. Her hands were on her hips and her chin was up and she was smiling. George kept on jigging, but his boots did not thump as loudly as they had thumped at first. Grandma's heels kept on clickety-clacking gaily. A drop of sweat dripped off George's forehead and shone on his cheek.

All at once he threw up both arms and gasped, "I'm beat!" He stopped jigging.

Everybody made a terrific noise, shouting and yelling and stamping, cheering Grandma. Grandma jigged just a little minute more, then she stopped. She laughed in gasps. Her eyes sparkled just like Pa's when he laughed. George was laughing, too, and wiping his forehead on his sleeve.

Suddenly Grandma stopped laughing. She turned and ran as fast as she could into the kitchen. The fiddle stopped playing. All the women were talking at once and all the men teasing George, but everybody was still for a minute, when Grandma looked like that.

Then she came to the door between the kitchen and the big room, and said: "The syrup is waxing. Come and help yourselves."

Then everybody began to talk and laugh again. They all hurried to the kitchen for plates, and outdoors to fill the plates with snow. The kitchen door was open and the cold air came in.

Outdoors the stars were frosty in the sky and the air nipped Laura's cheeks and nose. Her breath was like smoke.

She and the other Laura, and all the other children, scooped up clean snow with their plates. Then they went back into the crowded kitchen.

Grandma stood by the brass kettle and with the big wooden spoon she poured hot syrup on each plate of snow. It cooled into soft candy, and as fast as it cooled they ate it.

They could eat all they wanted, for maple sugar never hurt anybody. There was plenty of syrup in the kettle, and plenty of snow outdoors. As soon as they ate one plateful, they filled their plates with snow again, and Grandma poured more syrup on it.

When they had eaten the soft maple candy until they could eat no more of it, then they helped themselves from the long table loaded with pumpkin pies and dried berry pies and cookies and cakes. There was salt-rising bread, too, and cold boiled pork, and pickles. Oo, how sour the pickles were!

They all ate till they could hold no more, and then they began to dance again. But Grandma watched the syrup in the kettle. Many times she took a little of it out into a saucer, and stirred it round and round. Then she shook her head and poured the syrup back into the kettle.

The other room was loud and merry with the music of the fiddle and the noise of the dancing.

At last, as Grandma stirred, the syrup in the saucer turned into little grains like sand, and Grandma called:

"Quick, girls! It's graining!"

Aunt Ruby and Aunt Docia and Ma left the dance and came running. They set out pans, big pans and little pans, and as fast as Grandma filled them with the syrup they set out more. They set the filled ones away, to cool into maple sugar.

Then Grandma said:

"Now bring the patty-pans for the children."

There was a patty-pan, or at least a broken cup or a saucer, for every little girl and boy. They all watched anxiously while Grandma ladled out the syrup. Perhaps there would not be enough. Then somebody would have to be unselfish and polite.

There was just enough syrup to go round. The last scrapings of the brass kettle exactly filled the very last patty-pan. Nobody was left out.

The fiddling and the dancing went on and on. Laura and the other Laura stood around and watched the dancers. Then they sat down on

the floor in a corner, and watched. The dancing was so pretty and the music so gay that Laura knew she could never get tired of it.

All the beautiful skirts went swirling by, and the boots went stamping, and the fiddle kept on singing gaily.

Then Laura woke up, and she was lying across the foot of Grandma's bed. It was morning. Ma and Grandma and Baby Carrie were in the bed. Pa and Grandpa were sleeping rolled up in blankets on the floor by the fireplace. Mary was nowhere in sight; she was sleeping with Aunt Docia and Aunt Ruby in their bed.

Soon everybody was getting up. There were pancakes and maple syrup for breakfast, and then Pa brought the horses and sled to the door.

He helped Ma and Carrie in, while Grandpa picked up Mary and Uncle George picked up Laura and they tossed them over the edge of the sled into the straw. Pa tucked in the robes around them, and Grandpa and Grandma and Uncle George stood calling, "Good-by! Good-by!" as they rode away into the Big Woods, going home.

The sun was warm, and the trotting horses threw up bits of muddy snow with their hoofs. Behind the sled Laura could see their footprints, and every footprint had gone through the thin snow into the mud.

"Before night," Pa said, "we'll see the last of the sugar snow."

Old Log House

BY JAMES S. TIPPETT

Illustrated by Meg Wohlberg

On a little green knoll
At the edge of the wood
My great great grandmother's
First house stood.

The house was of logs
My grandmother said
With one big room
And a lean-to shed.

The logs were cut
And the house was raised
By pioneer men
In the olden days.

I like to hear
My grandmother tell
How they built the fireplace
And dug the well.

They split the shingles;
They filled each chink;
It's a house of which
I like to think.

Forever and ever
I wish I could
Live in a house
At the edge of a wood.

There Isn't Time

BY ELEANOR FARJEON

Illustrated by Meg Wohlberg

There isn't time, there isn't time,
To do the things I want to do,
With all the mountain-tops to climb,
And all the woods to wander through,
And all the seas to sail upon,
And everywhere there is to go,
And all the people, every one
Who lives upon the earth to know.
There's only time, there's only time,
To know a few, and do a few,
And then sit down and make a rhyme
About the rest I want to do.

The Stock Show

BY MEBANE HOLOMAN BURGWYN

Illustrated by Gertrude Howe

Allen and Bailey were rivals from the first day Bailey
came to Occoneechee Neck, North Carolina. No matter
how hard Allen tried, Bailey always won—in a fight, in a
school spelling contest, in everything. Allen wanted to win
just once. But most of all he wanted to win the
championship for the best calf in the 4-H contest. Training his calf, Lucky Mischief, and also hunting for an
escaped convict from the State Prison Farm made
this an exciting summer for Allen. Then came the day of
the 4H contest. Allen entered Lucky Mischief. Bailey
entered a calf, too. Who would win this time? Allen made
the most exciting discovery of all when the contest was over.

ALLEN WOKE to the sound of lowing cattle. Some of the boys
were already up feeding their steers. Allen put on the plaid shirt and
overalls over his clothes, then he put grain and cottonseed meal in
the bucket and spread some of the hay where his steer could get it.
While Lucky was eating Allen went outside to the soft drink stand
for a hamburger and milk for himself. When he came back he filled
the empty bucket with water from a hose outside the warehouse and
waited for Lucky to drink as much as he wanted.

The boy next to Allen untied his steer and led him out toward the
back of the building. By the time Lucky had finished drinking water,
the boy was back and had tied his steer to the fence again. He was
a big boy with a careless swinging walk. The light-colored steer was
beautiful and well built. The boy set down his bucket beside his steer
and began washing him with a brush and soapy water.

"I tried to get to the hose to wash Merry Pawnee with, but there
were two ahead of me and I just didn't want to stand around all
morning waiting."

At that moment Bailey came leading his steer back. Madcap had been washed clean with the hose.

Allen backed Lucky away from the fence and led him down the walkway out the back door of the building. He waited almost half an hour before he had a chance to use the hose. It was almost nine o'clock.

At last it was his turn. He wet Lucky thoroughly and then poured the liquid soap across his back. Then he scoured the steer with his brush from his head to each one of his four feet. He rubbed an extra amount of soap on the white tip of Lucky's tail and into the white hair on his face and down his back. When he was certain that Lucky was clean, Allen turned the hose on him and washed every trace of soap away. By this time Lucky was shivering from cold so Allen led him back inside to his place along the fence. He looked to see if his father had come yet. It was after nine now. People were coming into the warehouse, but Allen did not see Papa anywhere.

When he had tied Lucky, Allen brushed Lucky's hair down smooth against the side of his body. Then starting at the top of his back just below the center, Allen drew the teeth of his comb across the hair from Lucky's head to his tail. This left tiny ridges of turned hair the length of the steer's body. When Allen had finished the ridges he took the brush and brushed the hair up lightly. As the hair dried it left the hair looking neatly curled like a new permanent wave. Allen brushed the tail and then with clippers from the judges' desk he clipped the hair over Lucky's head. He was glad there were no horns to mar the smooth curve of the head.

Now Lucky was ready to be shown.

It was now almost ten o'clock. Allen wondered again if his father would get back in time for the show. The steer next to Allen, number three, suddenly kicked out his foot and threw wheat straw all over himself. Allen saw the boy's look of despair as he looked at the bits of straw all over the hair he had just brushed and curled. There was no way to get it off except to wash the steer again. And the judges were ready to begin.

"That's bad," said Allen to the boy. "I hope Lucky won't get the same idea."

He saw Papa and Mama come in and join the crowd that stood

around the area where the steers would be shown. Harry was with them. Allen waved to them and then a loud voice suddenly filled the building. An announcer at the desk was talking through a microphone. As he talked men placed benches around the open area for the judges and buyers to occupy.

"May I have your attention, please?" the announcer said.

Everyone stopped talking and listened. "The judges are now ready to judge the steers that the 4H members have brought here. The steers have been divided into three classes according to weight; the light weight group, the middle weight group, and the heavy weight group. From each group a champion will be chosen. He will receive a blue ribbon. The second best in each group will receive a red ribbon. The two best from each of these groups will enter the final contest for the grand champion award. The Champion will be awarded the purple ribbon. The reserve champion, or the second best in this group, will also receive a ribbon. All boys whose steers receive ribbons will receive a premium of fifteen dollars which has been donated to the 4H club by organizations which are interested in these shows and the boys who raise steers. The winner of the Grand Champion purple ribbon will not receive an extra prize but the steer will sell for the Champion's extra fancy price.

"Is everybody ready? Then will the boys who own the following steers bring them into the ring, please?"

He called out a series of numbers and Allen saw the boy next to him take Merry Pawnee out. It seemed only a minute before he was back holding a blue satin ribbon in his hand.

"You won first place," gasped Allen.

The boy grinned and then Allen was hearing his own number called out.

Allen turned to lead Lucky out. Lucky was lying down.

"Oh, Lucky, get up," he said. "Get up, Lucky."

But the steer would not budge.

The loud voice of the announcer again filled the building. "All right, boys, bring 'em out. Bring 'em out."

Allen begged and pulled and tugged at Lucky as the other boys led their steers out into the ring.

"All right," called the announcer. "Is this all?"

The judges started looking over the group of steers that were being held before them by the boys who owned them.

Allen was desperate. Lucky had not moved. Someone whispered something to the announcer for he called out, "There's one more steer, Judge. It seems he's taking a nap. He's so tired."

Everyone laughed.

"Well, get him out here," one of the judges said and there was no laughter in his voice.

Allen could have cried as he prodded Lucky.

"Come on. Come on there. Wake up," said the announcer.

Lucky suddenly heaved himself up and began to move slowly out into the ring as Allen touched him with his lead stick.

Allen went to the foot of the line and then touched Lucky's feet with the stick. Lucky placed his feet squarely under his body as he had been taught to do. But Allen could have cried out with despair for the hair that he had combed so carefully was now rough and tangled with straw on the side on which Lucky had been lying.

"Oh, Lucky, why did you have to lie down at the last minute?" he thought and watched as the judges looked at Lucky from all sides.

He almost groaned aloud when the judges, saying nothing, turned away from Lucky and looked at the next, smoothly groomed, animal.

In a moment one judge looked back at Lucky. "Take this one up to the head," the judge pointed to Lucky.

Allen's hopes leaped. He backed his steer out of the group and led Lucky around the back of the steers to the head of the line. He was now ahead of all the steers in his group.

The judge then pointed to another, "Take this one up to first place."

Lucky was now in second place. Number thirteen was first.

The judges moved out in front of the line and then back to the head. They looked carefully at Lucky and then at number thirteen. Number thirteen kept getting out of line. Lucky stood straight and still. Allen was glad of the time he had spent leading Lucky and training him to stand.

"But all his training won't do him any good if he can't win this first ribbon. He won't have a chance in the final show," Allen thought.

The judges moved out to one side. "Bring them out and walk them around," they ordered.

The boys led their steers out and led them in a circle around the judges. Allen held his breath when they looked at Lucky's rough side. "Put them back in line," the judges called. Then one of them came up and touched Lucky. "Put him first."

Allen backed Lucky out and led him around the steer that was in first place. Lucky was at the head of the line again. Allen's heart was beating harder now with hope, with hope, with hope. The judges ran their hands over Lucky's flesh and then they conferred among themselves.

The judges nodded, giving emphasis to the words one spoke, "That's the way they stand."

Allen stood straight while the announcer said the words that proclaimed Lucky the winner of the middle weight group. The officials came out and placed a blue ribbon in Allen's hand.

"Thank you, sir," he said and he could not help grinning with happiness as he led Lucky back to his place along the fence.

He passed Bailey taking his steer into the ring. Allen suddenly wondered if any of Bailey's folks were there to see if Bailey should win the blue ribbon for the heavy weight group.

It seemed only a moment before Allen heard the announcer say: "Winner of the first place in the heavy weight is number six, Madcap, exhibited by Bailey Mitchell of Northampton County. Boys, stay by your steers. The final contest will take place immediately."

Then the announcer was calling the numbers: 4, 5, 6, 10, 12, and 13. This was it; this was the final contest and now the real test between Allen and Bailey was to take place. The excitement of the moment was beating through the whole of Allen's body. For if he won, his victory would not only show that he had raised a better steer than Bailey but that he had raised a better steer than any boy in Northeastern North Carolina.

When the boys had placed their steers, Bailey's steer stood first, Lucky stood second and Merry Pawnee stood third. The other three were red ribbon winners in the first contests.

The judges stood before the six animals. Then they walked around and stood behind them. They examined each animal, feeling each carefully.

"Walk them around, boys," one of them said.

The boys led their steers out and walked around the ring. The judges watched them carefully. They already knew most of the good points from their examination in the preliminary contests.

"Put them back in line." The judges asked for no change in positions. Allen began to feel sick. When the steers stood still in line, the judges walked to the head of the line. They felt Madcap, pressed his sides and felt the legs. They examined the head and the feet.

Then they moved down to third place and examined Merry Pawnee. "Put him first," said one of the judges touching Merry Pawnee. Allen now stood in third place, Bailey in second. Allen felt hot tears of disappointment behind his eyelids but he fought them back and stood very straight.

The judges came to Lucky and felt him carefully. They looked at his face and ran their hands down his legs, over his back and sides, pressing, feeling Lucky's ribs that were well covered with a thick layer of high quality flesh. Lucky stood still, relaxed. The judges felt the solid strength and weight of him. Under their hands was the evidence of all of Allen's love and care and hope.

They backed away and began to talk to each other. At last one of them stepped up and touched Lucky. "Put him first," he said.

Allen's heart was suddenly flooded with a great joy. He backed Lucky out and placed him at the head of the line.

When Lucky stood still at the head of the line, the judges threw up their hands. "That's it," one of them said.

Allen's happiness caught in his throat. Lucky had won. The 4H contest was over and Lucky stood at the head of the line—Champion of the 4H show.

The voice of the announcer split through the buzz of conversation and activity of the warehouse. "Please, let me have your attention."

A silence followed.

"The judges have made their decisions. In the first place is the Champion, Lucky Mischief, Hereford steer weighing nine hundred seventy pounds, exhibited by Allen Peck of Occoneechee Neck, Northampton County."

Someone stepped up to Allen and placed a purple ribbon in his hand and on top of it a check for fifteen dollars because Lucky had been judged prime grade.

Breathless, Allen nodded his thanks. First place. Champion. The purple ribbon. Allen's heart beat hard against his ribs. He thought it must burst through with beating so hard and fast.

The crowd whistled and clapped and cheered. Allen grinned and grinned some more. Lucky stood placidly with a firm stance as became a winning steer.

The crowd pressed against Allen. A flash of light frightened him until he realized that a photographer had taken his picture. There was noise and confusion, people shook his hand, slapped him on the back and everybody was telling him how proud they were of his success.

Allen looked across the crowd straight into the eyes of Papa and he did not need any words to tell him how happy Papa was. The crease in his cheek was deep with his smile, and his eyes were steady with his pride. Mama was laughing and Harry was hopping up and down on one foot.

Allen led his steer back to the fence and tied him. 41

Now Allen was aware that the announcer was congratulating the owner of Merry Pawnee who had won second place. Bailey had not placed in the final contest at all.

Allen could not resist the urge to look over the heads of the crowd at Bailey.

Bailey's head was bent as he pushed his way through the crowd to take Madcap back to his place at the fence. He was tasting defeat at last. There could be no doubt in Bailey's mind now that Allen could do some things better.

After all the months of his defeat, Allen's victory was sweet. The triumph in his heart was a joyous one. He felt that he could stand on equal terms with Bailey now. Some of the tension of his antagonism toward Bailey began to ease. He wanted to laugh aloud.

But the laughter caught in his throat. Bailey Mitchell was walking toward him. He was looking straight into Allen's eyes, but he was not smiling. Allen stood with his feet apart and waited for Bailey.

Bailey stopped in front of Allen and stood for a moment not speaking. Allen waited. A fleeting thought crossed his mind once again. "I don't know anything about him. I don't know how his mind works." He remembered thinking this once before.

And then Bailey spoke. "I'm glad you won, Allen," he said.

Allen felt shocked to his very toes. He could not believe what he was hearing. Looking into Bailey's face, Allen knew he was not lying. Bailey meant what he was saying.

"Thanks, Bailey," Allen said and he looked down at his shoes.

They were new shoes, shiny brown shoes, but he did not see them. He was thinking of what Bailey had just said. Maybe he did not mean it the way it sounded. "How come you're glad I won, Bailey?"

"Well, my steer was just not good enough. I knew it as soon as I got here. And yours is the best one here. I don't know what the judges were worried about."

Into Allen's eyes and mind grew a spark of admiration for Bailey. It took a lot of courage for Bailey to come to him and say that. Bailey had lost this contest but he knew how to take it. For the first time Allen realized that only a really good fellow could lose and then give sincere congratulations to the winner. Bailey was a good loser and a good fellow. Allen began to feel a warmth, a friendliness toward Bailey rising within him. It was a growth of the warm feeling he had felt last night when he cured Bailey's steer. He wanted to tell Bailey how he felt for he believed that Bailey might like to be friends with him and searched for the right words to say.

"Aw shucks, Bailey," he said finally and the boys looked at each other.

There was a moment full of things they wished to say and did not know how to say and then Papa and Mama came up with Harry. Their greeting swept him away from Bailey and he was soon out of the building, eating lunch with them without having said to Bailey any of the things that he had felt.

By one o'clock, Allen was back in the warehouse. In half an hour the sale would begin and after that he would be going home. Mama and Papa had gone downtown to shop so they could leave right after the sale.

Allen thought he would like to walk over to the unused part of the building and look at the great tobacco barrels that were stacked there. He rubbed his lead stick down Lucky's back for a moment. "I'll be back in a minute, Lucky. I'm just wondering if those barrels are as big as they look."

He crossed the sunken driveway and walked into the dimness of 43 the other side of the building which was closed. The barrels were stacked in rows with narrow spaces between. After the noise of the other side of the building it seemed quiet, and dark and creepy. A dampness permeated the air making it seem chilly.

Allen began to think that he had seen enough and had turned to go back when something stopped him. There was someone talking. The hushed sound of voices pricked at his ears.

Someone was saying, "Hush, hush, boy." And then he heard the sound of muffled sobbing.

Allen was unable to control the impulse that drew him toward the sound. Something was wrong and he could not leave without knowing what it was. He crept closer until the sound was quite near. He peered around the curve of one of the barrels and saw, only a few feet from him, the slender body of Bailey, leaning against one of the barrels and Bailey was crying. Beside him stood an enormous man saying, "Hush."

Something familiar about the man filled Allen with sudden horror and then the man turned slightly giving Allen a good view of his face. It was the convict. The very convict he had locked in his house yesterday. He looked in the dimness as though he might be clean and shaven and dressed in different clothes, but it was the same man, Allen was certain.

The man reached out his hand and put it on Bailey's shoulder.

"I'm not going to do it. I'm not going to do it," Bailey sobbed.

Allen drew back for a moment. Bailey was in trouble. The convict was trying to make Bailey do something. That was clear. Perhaps he meant to harm Bailey. No, it was more likely that the convict wanted Bailey to help him get away and Bailey was refusing.

Allen felt that at last he was on the verge of clearing up the mysterious connection of Bailey and the escaped convicts. But of one thing he was certain, Bailey was in trouble and perhaps in danger and he needed help quickly.

Allen looked at the lead stick in his hand. "I could hurt that man enough so that Bailey could get away and call for help," he thought.

He looked up at the tall barrel beside him, thinking, and then holding the stick between his teeth he leaped up, caught the rim of the barrel and scrambled onto it. Then he stepped carefully across the spaces until he stood directly above and behind Bailey and the man with him.

For a moment he stood there poised to jump down on the huge man. "I'll jump with all my weight. The surprise may knock him off his feet." Then he crouched to leap.

"But, Daddy," said Bailey, "there is bound to be some other way."

Allen, standing on the edge of the barrel, heard only the one word "Daddy." The impulse to leap was stopped in mid air by the shock of Bailey's word. He fell in amazement at the feet of Bailey and his father.

He was conscious that Bailey screamed and that the father uttered an oath of surprise and then they were helping him to his feet.

"Allen," said Bailey, "where did you fall from?" He looked up into the dark maze of rafters overhead.

"No," said Allen. "Not up there. I was on the barrel."

The big man bent and looked into his face and then he straightened. Allen drew back in fright. The man had recognized him.

"This is my father, Allen. He works as a special investigator for the State."

For a moment Allen could not speak. In his astonishment his mouth flew open and remained so while he stared at the man. It was the same man all right.

"Then you're not a—the—con——?" his voice trailed off.

The man laughed. "I'm the man you locked up, all right, but I'm not the convict. The State had me down in the Neck trying to find out why so many convicts are getting away."

Allen closed his mouth and swallowed. An investigator. And he had locked this man up.

"Did you find out?" he asked weakly.

"Well, no. And you certainly didn't help me out any. I had been tramping those woods for two days when I came to your house looking for Bailey. I couldn't find him at home."

Allen's surprise turned to embarrassment and shame. He had not only locked this man up and probably kept him from finding out what he had gone to the Neck to discover, but he had almost attacked him

45

with his lead stick as well.

"Gosh, Capt'n Mitchell, I sure am sorry I locked you up. You didn't tell me who you were." Out of deep respect Allen gave this man a title.

"The dickens I didn't. I yelled at you for ten minutes after you locked me in that kitchen and I thought I'd never get through that kitchen window."

He suddenly began laughing big, deep, hearty laughter, that matched his size. He shook with it. It filled the warehouse and rang through the rafters above. It seemed to clear the damp musty air. Allen and Bailey began laughing, too. They moved out through the spaces between the barrels laughing.

"You should have seen me trying to squeeze through that little window after I couldn't stop you. I knew I had to be in Rocky Mount last night and I did not know when you would come back, so I just had to get out." His laughter came more quietly now. "If I had been as small as the convict who got away, it wouldn't have been a bit of trouble, but I thought I'd never get out."

Allen remembered his suspicion of Bailey. "Well, tell me, Capt'n Mitchell, did you see anything of my steer when you got out of that window?"

"Your steer? No." Then he paused. "Come to think of it, I did see a woman leading a steer near the woods, though."

Allen's eyes flew open and he looked at Bailey.

"An old woman?"

"Well, I couldn't tell how old she was. She had on a bright colored skirt."

"Miss Ida," gasped Allen. "Miss Ida must have taken him out. But why?" And in his surprise a faint memory began to nag his thoughts. "There's something about this I ought to remember, something important," but the idea escaped him.

Bailey had been listening in amazement to all the conversation. "I didn't know about all of that," he said.

"No," said his father. "I lost so much time at Allen's that I couldn't go back to see you. I had to meet the fellow who was to come to the Neck for me. And that reminds me, I have to go now. But I will see you again tonight, Bailey. I am coming to the Neck to see Uncle Tom for a little while."

Bailey looked at his father and for a minute Allen thought he might cry again but he did not. Instead he said softly, "Bye, Dad."

And the big man walked out of the big entrance doors of the warehouse. Allen and Bailey walked back toward their steers. The big clock said there was still some time to wait before the sale.

"I reckon you wondered why I was crying," said Bailey.

"Sure," said Allen. "I thought he was a convict. I thought he was trying to hurt you."

Bailey looked quickly at Allen. "And you were going to fight him?" There was appreciation in his eyes but he went on talking. "He had just told me that I will have to come back here and live with my aunt. You see, I don't want to leave the Neck."

"Do you have to leave?"

"Yeah. Dad has been trying to make enough money to straighten out all the debts that Uncle Tom owes on the farm in the Neck. The old man wants us to come live with him but he's about to lose the farm because there's no money to pay all he owes. Now that I lost the 4H show and the chance to sell Madcap for a good price and Dad's lost the convict, we've lost our chance to live in the Neck and we'll have to come back and live here with Aunt Drew." His eyelids dropped for a moment but Allen saw the glint beneath them. "Aunt Drew is a devil and she makes things awful for me and Dad, specially for me." His voice was low.

"Gee," said Allen, "that's bad."

"You see Mama died about three years ago. We lived in the mountains on account of her bad health, and after she died—" Bailey paused and bent his head but then he lifted it again and went on talking as though he were talking to himself. "Well, things just don't seem to turn out right. Dad wants to get back on the farm. He's been working for the State since we came here. And when the State offered him a bonus along with the reward if he could find out why or how the convicts were getting away, he thought maybe we could make it."

"Oh," said Allen. "I reckon I understand a lot of things now." He thought of his own home—of Mama's good meals and gay ways, of   47

Papa's kindness, of Harry and Jenny. Bailey had nobody but his daddy and no home that even the two of them could share.

"I wanted to help," said Bailey, "so he gave me Madcap to enter in this contest. I tried to help him find the convicts, too. I was looking for footprints when you saw me on the river bank that day."

"Oh," said Allen again. "And you were mad when I saw you."

"I was afraid you might know what I was doing. Dad said I couldn't tell a soul what he was doing because he could work better if nobody knew, but I had to keep to myself all the time, I was so afraid I would let out a little bit of the secret.

"I couldn't even see him often. But he nearly always came to see me when he was down there hunting for the convicts. I hung around waiting, hoping he'd come. I got kinda lonesome."

"Was that why you ran home the day we had the rock muddle?" asked Allen.

"Yeah. I went home both days that we had the rock muddles. Last year and yesterday, too. I met you on the road yesterday."

"Yeah, I know. That was right after I locked your daddy up," said Allen.

Again the strange feeling that he must remember something that he had forgotten began to bother Allen. He rubbed his head trying to think. Bailey continued, "That day you saw me at Blue Hole I had been following a man I had never seen before. I still think he was the second convict. But then I ran into the hornets' nest and he got away."

"I thought you stirred up those hornets on purpose," said Allen. "I just wish I had known what you were really doing. I would have helped you."

"I thought you didn't like me," Bailey said.

"Well," said Allen sheepishly, "to tell the truth, I reckon I didn't, but mostly it was because I didn't know you. If I'd known all these things I would have liked you anyway."

The two boys looked at each other again. Facing the truth they realized that they liked each other very much and that while they might be rivals in their activities, there would still be this warm feeling of friendship between them.

Share and Share Alike

BY ELEANOR ESTES

Illustrated by Louis Slobodkin

To live in Cranbury on New Dollar Street, to have a mother
who could just make ends meet and have fun doing it,
to be one of a family of four children (four is such a
handy number because it is easy to divide things evenly),
all this meant fun, laughter, and love to those Moffats—
Joey, Sylvie, Jane, and Rufus M. Here is the story
of one day's adventuring with Jane.

At LAST the terrific cold weather had gone. Now it was spring. The
ground was soft and spongy and the lilacs were in bloom. Jane sat on
the hitching post, carefully holding in her moist palm the first few
violets she had just found and watching Joe and Rufus. They were over
in front of the yellow house practicing on their stilts. Of course Joe
was doing very well, but Rufus found that walking on stilts was quite
a lot more difficult than just walking on his own two legs. On stilts his
legs kept going wider and wider apart all the time so that he had to
jump off and begin all over again. Jane couldn't help it; she had to
laugh at him. He looked so funny. But Rufus didn't care.

Now and then Joe rested against the front of the yellow house.
Once he leaned against the For Sale sign.

"That old sign!" he muttered.

"Why don't you tear it down?" asked Jane, responding to Joe's
irritation.

"Can't. But I'll fix it up a bit," said Joe. He took a red chalk from
his pocket and changed the S into a $ sign.

Jane looked at his work in silent approval. The For Sale sign was weather-beaten and dingy but it most certainly was still there. Now that the warm weather had arrived, a few prospective buyers had come to examine the house. Mama said she would look for another house for them to live in. She didn't like living in a house that might be sold over her head at any minute. But the children begged her not to move until they really had to. "Maybe no one will buy it," they said. For the sign had been there a long time and no one had bought the yellow house yet.

Jane swung around on the hitching post. Of all the houses on New Dollar Street, theirs was the only one with a For Sale sign on it. Why did it have to be *their* house? Because it was the best one, of course.

Now she watched Mr. Brooney, the grocery man, drive up with his horse and wagon. The Moffats called Mr. Brooney's horse the dancey horse because of the graceful way he threw his legs about when he cantered up the street. Mr. Brooney stopped between Mrs. Squire's house and the yellow house. He threw down the heavy iron weight to keep his horse from dancing away and took several baskets of groceries from the wagon. He crossed the street and disappeared in Mrs. Frost's back yard. He was gone a long time. The horse stood there with the greatest patience. Occasionally he flicked his long tail to rid himself of a pesky fly. Or now and then he wriggled an ear when Sylvie, who was practicing her graduation music, hit a high note. And sometimes he raised one dainty foot or another and then planted it firmly on the ground. For the most part, however, he stood there dreamily, looking neither to left or to right.

Jane watched him and watched him.

He had wings and could carry her away.

He was the wooden horse of Troy and many men could step out of him.

He was a bridge that she could walk under.

Sitting up there on the hitching post, watching the horse and watching the horse, Jane repeated to herself, "The horse is a bridge for me to walk under, and I'm goin' to walk under it."

So she jumped down and marched over to the horse. He stood there immobile. Except for his eyes which followed her around like those

of the velvet-clad lady in the picture in the sitting-room.

Jane walked under him and came out on the other side. This gave her an extraordinary feeling of satisfaction and elation.

At that moment when Jane was walking under the horse, Mama came to the window of the front parlor and shook her duster out vigorously. "Thank heavens!" she said to herself; "thank heavens, it's spring again and that long hard winter is over." No more fussing with stoves and wondering where the next coal was coming from, she thought, slapping the duster against the green shutters. And better still, there was lots of work to do. Tilly Cadwalader was getting married. Mama had not only the bridal outfit to make but the bridesmaids' gowns too. The yellow house was just bulging with white satin and tulle, with billowy yellow and lavender tulle. It was to be a really elegant affair that would keep her busy and the pantry full for some time, she thought with satisfaction.

But goodness! Could Mama believe her eyes? What was Janey doing? Walking under that horse! Of all things! Mama was speechless with amazement and dropped the duster out of the window at the sight. Joe and Rufus saw her from the other side of the yard and became all tangled up in their stilts in consequence. Sylvie, who was practicing her singing way back in the kitchen, was the only one who did not see her.

"Jane! Whatever on earth!" Mama cried. "You mustn't do such things. You mustn't walk under horses. They might kick or start walking or something."

Jane stepped thoughtfully up the walk. "All right, Mama," she said.

She had no desire to keep on walking under horses. It was just something she felt she had to do at that moment, just that once. And she knew that horse. She'd been watching him and watching him. So she had walked under him and from the feeling inside of her she thought it had turned out to be an all right sort of thing to do—just that once.

Joe and Rufus resumed their stilt-walking. Their sister Jane sometimes did extremely curious things, they agreed.

Mama called to Jane to hand her her duster. Mama was still disturbed about Jane walking under that horse. Of course she was used to unexpected things happening. After all, with four such children that was only natural. But walking under a horse, now! That was different and dangerous. It is true that Jane herself had no further desire or interest in walking under a horse again. But Mama had no way of knowing this. Goodness! For all she knew, Jane might make a habit of this. Best send her on some errand and get her mind off horses.

"Jane," she said, "run down the street to Tilly Cadwalader's and ask her to just slip on this sleeve for the length."

Mama carefully wrapped the sleeve in white tissue paper. She told Jane not to run and to be very careful. If anything happened to that sleeve, she didn't know what she'd do because there wasn't any more satin and goodness only knows . . . "Why, maybe Tilly couldn't get married at all if anything happens to this sleeve, and that would be a dreadful thing, a dreadful thing altogether," said Mama, chuckling.

Jane took the package and walked as carefully up the street as though she were carrying a lemon meringue pie. The Cadwaladers lived in a sleepy-looking gray house across the street from Chief Mulligan's. The shingles protruded over each window like languorous, drooping eyelids. "I bet they close like eyes after everyone has gone to bed," thought Jane, grinning to herself as she rang the bell. There was a good deal of suspense in ringing the Cadwaladers' bell. There were seven Cadwalader sisters. Of course you never knew which one of them would open the door. When the door opened, you had the excitement of thinking fast to say the right Hello: Hello, Tilly, Hello, Milly, Hello, Molly, Polly, Lollie, or Hello, Olly. And last, Hello, Nelly. "Like the game of beast, bird or fish almost," laughed Jane as the door swung open.

This time it was "Hello, Tilly," the eldest and the only Cadwalader girl who wore her hair high on her head.

Jane stepped into the front parlor. She snuffed the air here. This house had a different sort of smell altogether from the yellow house. She handed the sleeve to Tilly. Tilly tried it on. The six other sisters stood around saying Oh, and Ah. Milly Cadwalader wanted to see how Tilly would look as a bride. She snatched down one of the lace curtains and held it on Tilly's head. Yes, she was a bride with the satin sleeve and the lace curtain on. All the sisters clapped their hands and laughed and one thumped "Here comes the bride" on the small organ.

Then Milly, Lollie, Polly, Olly and last of all, little Nelly, had each one to play at being the bride. When this was done, Tilly carefully folded the sleeve into the tissue paper again and then she reached for the bank that stood between a Dresden shepherd and his shepherdess. This bank was made out of an orange.

"How did you ever make it?" marveled Jane politely.

"Just scooped out the insides," said Tilly carelessly. She skillfully coaxed out a nickel for Jane with a nail file.

"There," she said. "Thank you so much for coming way down here with the sleeve. Tell your mother it fits beautifully and looks beautiful. You think she will surely have everything ready on time?"

"Oh, yes," replied Jane. "I'm helpin' with the bastings."

Jane was anxious to be off. The nickel burned in her pocket. As she said good-by to all the Cadwalader girls who waved their handkerchiefs and aprons after her, she was thinking about all the good things a nickel can buy.

She raced home with the sleeve. She handed it to Mama who was sewing now in the Grape Room. Sylvie was working in her small patch of vegetable garden which she had planted just the day before. Joe and Rufus had disappeared somewhere with their stilts. Jane clutched the nickel tightly in her fist and walked slowly up the street. She stopped in the Brick Lot to see if any more violets were up yet. There were three with lovely long stems! She picked these and continued on her way down the street towards the railroad tracks. She was going to Mr. Brooney's store. She would surprise them all with something awfully good.

It was lucky there were four of them, she thought. Everything divided so beautifully into four parts. Sylvie, Joe, Jane, and Rufus could not imagine how it would feel if there were just three of them, or five of them, or any other number of them. Imagine having to divide into three parts like the Pudges. Or seven like the Cadwaladers! "I suppose they are used to it, though," she thought. But this way, having four in the family, everything was so easy. Cut a piece of chocolate into four parts. No difficulty at all. Or there was one apiece of four-for-a-penny caramels; or a half apiece of two-for-a-penny peppermints. Yes, it was very convenient having four in the family. "When we grow up we shall each have four children," said Jane to herself, "so things will always be easy to divide." Share and share alike was the rule of the Moffat household and no one ever thought to dispute it.

And now there was this five cents from Tilly Cadwalader. Think of all the fine things it might buy. Twenty caramels, ten sticks of licorice, one ice-cream cone—but that was foolish. An ice-cream cone cannot be divided. Ten peppermint patties, four sheets of paper dolls, one ice-cream cone. "One ice-cream cone" danced before her eyes. It was a hot day for May. It would be nice to taste your first ice-cream cone on a day like this when you had also found your first violets. Oh, if that five cents would only grow into four five cent pieces.

But here she was at Brooney's. Somehow or other her feet marched

her right over to the ice-cream counter. No more hesitating over what that nickel was going to buy. Something inside had decided for her. A small, thin voice—Jane knew it was none of hers—said, "One ice-cream cone, please. Strawberry."

Jane sat on the bread-box, kicking her legs against the sides. The ice-cream cone was absolutely delicious. At least the first few bites were delicious. But the more she ate, the less she enjoyed it. She was a pig, that's what, a pig. She found she couldn't eat the last few bites of the cone at all. She gave it to Mr. Brooney's little yellow dog, Jup, who gobbled it up without the least trace of enthusiasm, as though he were doing her a favor in fact.

She sat there disconsolately for some minutes. The few violets she had picked had wilted in her moist hand. She gave them to little Gretta Brooney who was delighted with them. Jane banged her feet against the bread-box. She thought of the bag of sweets she might have had. She could have surprised them all! How pleased and excited everyone would have been. Instead of that she was nothing but an old pig. She started for home, thoroughly ashamed and angry with herself. None of the others would have done such a thing. Well, she never would again, of that she was sure.

When she reached home, she found that even Catherine-the-cat had been faithful to the share and share alike principle and had brought four new little kittens to the yellow house. Catherine brought four kittens every year, one for each of the Moffat children. This year she had hidden them in the barn until they were old enough to hold up their wobbly heads and stand on their shaky legs. So on this day she had brought them into the yellow house for Mama to see.

Mama found an old wooden soap-box for them and there they were, wagging their heads when Jane came in. Sylvie, Joe, and

Rufus were all sitting on the floor watching them.

"We been waitin' for you," said Rufus, beside himself with excitement. "We're going to do the choosing now."

Choosing their kitten was a game they played every year. This was great sport, the only sad thing about it being the thought that they would have to part with their new pets as soon as Mama could find homes for them. This was never difficult, for there wasn't a better mouser in the whole town of Cranbury than Catherine and it was expected that her kittens would inherit this skill.

"Oh, aren't they cunning?" gasped Jane as Sylvie lifted each one of them out of the box.

The kittens would try to stand on their shaking legs. But this was very hard for them and every few minutes they would fall into sitting positions. There they would remain for a time, heads wobbling foolishly from side to side. Then they would try again this exciting business of walking. The four kittens seemed quite bewildered at all the strange people, the strange world. All except one. This one, a ball of gray fuzz, with perfectly enormous feet, leaped into the air a few times and then started on a tour of exploration. Every few steps she would fall down. But she kept right on trying. There was no doubt that this kitten was the most enterprising of the four.

Rufus burst out laughing at her. "Gee, I hope I win that one," he said.

That was what they all hoped. The little gray one was the favorite.

"Oh, let this one be mine," Jane prayed, although she felt she didn't deserve any such luck after spending that whole five cents on herself.

The children looked the kittens over and decided on temporary names for them. The little gray one they called Boots because of her truly extraordinary feet. Another kitten they named Mask. This one was black all over except for its face, which was white. It was Rufus who thought up the name Mask for it. Another they called Whiskers and the last one they named Funny because she had one green eye and one blue eye. Next Sylvie wrote each of these names on four pieces of paper. These she dropped into Mama's hat.

56 "Now, who will be the one to draw out the names?" Sylvie asked.

"Rufus! Rufus!" cried Joe and Janey. "Because he is the littlest."

"All right," said Sylvie. "Whichever cat has his name drawn by Rufus will be set in the middle of the room. Then we will all go to the four different corners of the room and call, Kitty, Kitty. Whichever person that kitten goes to, why, that person will be the winner of that kitten."

Sylvie had thought this game up years ago and they all loved it.

So now Rufus closed his eyes, put his chubby fist into the hat, and drew out the first name. They waited with bated breath while Sylvie read the name.

"Funny!" she said.

A cheer went up as Funny was put in the middle of the room.

"Kitty, kitty, kitty," the children called from the four corners of the room. In this game it was possible that you might have a preference for one or another of the four kittens. But this must never be evident. You must call as fervently for this one as that one.

"Kitty, kitty, kitty," they called to the little one named Funny.

"Mu-u-r-r." A very feeble, wistful cry came from Funny. She turned around with difficulty. She was feeling terribly alone in a strange world. Suddenly she rushed as fast as she could towards Jane. However, walking in a straight line was utterly impossible for her and it was Sylvie's corner she finally ended up in. So Sylvie and Funny were out of the game.

Rufus scrunched up his face, put his hand in the hat again. The name was—Whiskers!

Whiskers! Cheers again. But Whiskers didn't care. He just sat there with his head nodding on his shoulders, looking as though he were going to fall asleep at any moment.

"Kitty, kitty, kitty," Joe, Jane, and Rufus coaxed.

Whiskers just sat there and looked around the room with a pleasant though simple expression.

"Come, Whiskers. Come, kitty," they pleaded again.

But Whiskers just sat there, swaying gently to and fro.

"We shall have to go nearer to this one," said Joey in the manner of a patient parent.

Joey, Jane, and Rufus drew nearer, to within a few feet of Whiskers. Still he just sat.

"He doesn't want to play," said Rufus in disgust.

Now the three went right up close to him. Just a kitten's length away. At this, Whiskers stood up on his shaky legs and staggered nonchalantly over to Rufus. He nestled comfortably on his sleeve and was asleep in a second. So Rufus and Whiskers were out of the game too.

Now just Boots and Mask were left. And Joe and Jane.

"Oh, please let Boots be mine," Jane prayed again and again. "Although of course I know I don't deserve it," she added.

Rufus drew again. This time the name was—Boots.

Boots! The children all cheered lustily. Boots herself seemed full of excitement. All the while the game had been going on, she had been clawing at the soap box and miaowing madly to get out. Now she was out!

"Oh, be mine, be mine," breathed Jane.

"Look at the big toes on her," Joe marveled. "Boy, oh, boy, I hope I win her."

Of course Joe was just as anxious for Boots as Jane was. And why shouldn't he be? Of these four sweet kittens she alone showed marks of personality that lifted her above the usual run of cats and kittens. She paid no attention to Joe or to Jane. Instead she raced madly around the room. She whacked at a tassel that was hanging from the red plush chair. This caused her to lose her balance and she rolled over and over. Up again. She resumed her swift, though wobbly, adventuring through the sitting-room, the new world.

"Oh, pussy, come. Come, pussy," Jane begged.

Boots ran right over to Jane's corner but then, just as she was within a cat's length of her, she backed off to the middle of the room. What a kitten!

"Come, kitty, come, kitty," said Joey in that gentle voice of his that surely Boots would not be able to resist.

Now Boots teetered over towards Joe. She sat down not far from him and stared at him with her big blue eyes. Her little pink tongue was hanging out and she was thoroughly irresistible. Suddenly she began to purr. She was the first one to purr and she sounded like a little engine.

"She's going to Joey," mourned Jane. "Well, of course I don't deserve her."

But at this moment Boots suddenly turned right about again. She jumped wildly into the air a couple of times and then, in a series of little sidewise leaps, she landed right in Jane's lap. Tears came into Jane's eyes. "She's mine. She's mine," she cried, burying her nose in Boots' sweet-smelling fur.

So Mask went to Joey and he immediately found many engaging things about this kitten that they had not yet discovered. For instance, he had the longest fur, the prettiest markings, the longest tail, and many other unusual qualities. Moreover he was the smallest of the four and would need special attention.

At this moment Catherine-the-cat came in. She looked around the room disdainfully. Then she jumped into the soap-box and whirrupped for her kittens. Janey gave Boots one last hug. She already

59

loved this little kitten so much it was almost more than she could bear. She put the kitten carefully back into the soap-box as the other children were doing with theirs. And the choosing game was over.

Joe and Rufus went back to the yard to continue their stilt walking. Sylvie went into the Grape Room to help Mama with the Tilly Cadwalader wedding dress. Janey went out to the big old lilac bush at the side of the house. What a mixed-up sort of day it had been! This day she had walked under a horse, been a pig about an ice-cream cone, and won Boots, the sweetest of all kittens, though she didn't deserve it.

Jareb and the Contest

BY MIRIAM POWELL

Illustrated by Marc Simont

His name was Jareb, but most folks in the pine woods
of Georgia called him Jeb. Jeb loved the tall pines,
and he dreamed of having pine seedlings of his own
to give to his father for a Christmas gift. But
how could he get them when he had no money? When
Mr. Calhoun's tree-planting contest came along, Jeb
had his chance. He knew he could win—if he
didn't care *how* he won. Could there be something
more important than winning? Jeb finds out—and you
will find out too as you read his story.

LITTLE LIJE Moody was a thin, puny boy, younger than Jeb and small for his age. It was hard to believe he was any kin at all to his older brother Mose, for Little Lije was mostly quiet and shy. He handled the pine plants as if he had a feeling for them, and somehow Jeb knew without being told that he wanted mighty bad to win those seedlings.

Mr. Calhoun had divided the rest of the acreage into five sections, staking off and marking the plots so that each of the boys could be assigned to one. Jeb and Little Lije were side by side, the other three boys a short distance away, separated from them by ground already planted the day before.

"Boy! Wouldn't hit be fine to have them seedlin's, though?" said Little Lije as they settled down to work.

"I mean hit would," agreed Jeb, lifting his grub hoe to make the first hole. "I figure to git 'em, too," he added.

Little Lije sighed. "I wisht I could. I could plant 'em right out on the land Pa promised to give me. I'm the onliest one to our house that likes to grow things," he explained. "But I reckon me and you ain't hardly got a chance."

"How come?" asked Jeb, although he knew well enough what the other boy meant.

Little Lije looked over at his brother and the Crump boys.

"Well, Sol won't be no hindrance," he said, "all he wants is to git his pay. But hit's somethin' else again with Mose and Hezzie. Don't neither one of 'em care shucks about the seedlin's, but they aim to win 'em jest the same."

Jeb glanced at the two older boys and his fingers tightened around the handle of his grub hoe.

"So do I," he declared and went earnestly to work. He had to get ahead of Mose and Hezzie somehow; he just had to. It would be easy to beat them if he hurried, poking the plants into the ground just any old way. But much as he wanted those seedlings for Paw, he couldn't bring himself to cheat on Mr. Calhoun or the plants. Those young trees had a right to a good start.

As he worked Jeb remembered what the boss had told them the day before. Each hole should be deep enough so the long taproot would have plenty of room, wide enough for the smaller roots to spread. The soil must be packed twice before the hole was filled, then gently firmed with his foot before he could leave that plant to go on to the next. And all the time the seedlings in the bucket had to be kept wet around the roots until the young trees were put into the ground.

Jeb was too busy most of the morning to pay much mind to any of the others. It was nearly noon before he noticed that Little Lije was having trouble. He was way behind on his planting.

"What's the matter, Lije?" he asked.

"Seems like this here grub hoe must be conjured," said the boy. "I cain't figure what ails hit.'

Jeb hefted the hoe. "This ain't no grub hoe," he said. "Hit's a mattock." No wonder Little Lije couldn't handle it. The mattock was more cumbersome than a grub hoe, too heavy even for Jeb to use with ease.

"I ain't scared of no conjure," said Jeb. "I'll swap with you." He fetched his grub hoe and traded with Little Lije. "Better make them holes a little bigger now, so's the roots can stretch and grow good," he advised.

"I will," said Little Lije. "Reckon you can work all right with that there mattock?"

"I can make out good," Jeb declared and went on back to his job.

It took the rest of that week, right up to noon of the day before Christmas Eve, to finish the work for Mr. Calhoun. Jeb couldn't keep from thinking how fine it would be to have those seedlings as a present for Paw, even though he knew now there was no hope of beating Mose and Hezzie. Both older boys were running a neck-and-neck race, far ahead of what Jeb had been able to do. The heavy old mattock held him back considerably, but he had to admit to himself that even with the lighter grub hoe he could never have kept up the pace set by the older boys. Doggedly he kept on, bound to finish the best he could. He'd get paid for the week's work, anyway. There'd have to be some other kind of Christmas present for Paw.

On the last day Mr. Calhoun sent a man down to keep an eye on the work they were doing to see which one of the boys finished his share of the planting first. Mose turned out to be the winner, and a few minutes later Hezzie planted the last tree needed to cover his plot. The best Jeb could do was to finish next; Sol and Little Lije came last.

As soon as Mose had finished he came swaggering over to watch Jeb and Little Lije, after making sure Foreman Sam knew he'd won the contest.

"I got money and I got trees," bragged Mose. "Reckon I'll have to hire one of you young'uns to set out my seedlin's for me."

Jeb was surprised to hear Little Lije speak up. He might be puny, but he wasn't scared of his overgrown big brother.

"You don't want them trees no more'n Sol does, Mose Moody, and you know hit good as I do," he said. He was like a spunky little sparrow jumping on a jaybird. "You won't be hirin' nobody to set 'em out, neither—you got nowhere to plant 'em!"

"I don't know about that," said Mose. "I'm the one's got the seedlin's, remember. Wouldn't surprise me none did Pa decide to give me that there land he said you could have. You got nothin' to plant on hit, small fry; I have."

The fire died right out of Little Lije, and his eyes seemed bigger and sadder than ever. "Pa wouldn't!" he choked. "He promised hit to me."

Jeb leaned against his mattock and, ignoring Mose, turned to the younger boy. "Forget it, Lije," he said. "You got money now to buy some with, ain't you?" Little Lije nodded without enthusiasm. "Not only that, I know how you and me can git all the seedlin's we crave without payin' nobody nothin' for 'em. Mr. Calhoun was tellin' me all about hit." He wasn't as sure of what he was saying as he made out, but it was worth it to see how Little Lije brightened up.

"Well, lookit who's talkin'!" sneered Mose. "Toady-boy Judson, Calhoun's pet. Ain't man enough to win in a contest, fair and square, so he works behind our backs to git trees from the boss anyways."

Jeb was outraged. "I never done nothin' of the kind," he declared. He knew he couldn't match words with Mose, but he was too mad to keep his mouth shut.

"Prove hit, then," challenged Mose, and Jeb didn't say any more. He couldn't prove it, not without going to Mr. Calhoun, and that was the last thing he wanted to do. Lifting his mattock, he went back to work, his face on fire and his chest tight with fury.

Mose still hung around, watching. "No wonder you're so fur behind, toady-boy," he said to Jeb. "How come you to handle them plants like that? They ain't gonna break."

Jeb didn't answer, and Mose went on. "Treat 'em a little rough, young'un. They can take it—same as the women. You don't treat your gal like you do them plants, do you?"

Jeb couldn't keep from answering that one. It purely riled him to have this big bully making fun of Dovey Tatum.

"She ain't my gal," he said. "She's my friend."

Mose slapped his thigh and laughed so loud that Hezzie came over to see what was going on. Hezzie had finished by now, too.

"Hey, Hez, listen to the young'un, will ya?" he howled. "Says he ain't got no gal; she's jest his friend," he mimicked. Both boys started laughing and joking then, until Foreman Sam came and ran them off.

"Git goin', boys," he said. "Leave the young'uns be. The boss wants this work finished this evenin'; they won't never git done long as you keep pesterin' 'em."

"Don't pay Mose no mind, Jeb," said Little Lije as the older boys went on off. "He all the time carries on that-a-way. He don't mean nothin' by it."

Jeb forced a smile at the little fellow. "Mose jest likes to hear hisself talk, I reckon," he said, but a lump clogged his throat. He sure did want those seedlings, and seeing them go to Mose was a whole lot worse than losing them to anybody else. He wondered if maybe Mose would sell the young plants—he'd be bound to care more about the money than the trees. Hope surged briefly through Jeb, them died. He couldn't use his money that way. Not with Lissy needing all   65 those special things they had to buy; not with Christmas coming.

Still trying to think of a way out and busy getting his last few trees in the ground, Jeb didn't hear Mr. Calhoun come up behind him. He didn't know the boss was there until he spoke.

"Does me a sight of good to watch you work, boy," he said to Jeb. "You've got a way with trees; I can tell by the way you handle those seedlings."

Warm happiness spread through Jeb's insides. It was nearly as good as winning to get such praise from Mr. Calhoun.

"Hit pleasures me to plant 'em," he said.

"You've done a good job, son. Jud Judson ought to be proud of you," said Mr. Calhoun as he walked away. Jeb heard him admire the way Little Lije had his trees set up, but as far as he could tell the boss had nothing to say as he examined the crop planted by Mose and Hezzie.

The two older boys came sauntering back while the boss was talking to the foreman.

"All right, boys, guess we're all here now," said Mr. Calhoun as the boys formed a group around him. "Sam here is all set to pay you off, but we've got some other business to attend to first." It was the prize he was talking about, the leftover seedlings that Mose had won. Mose was leaning against a fence post chewing on a piece of sour grass and looking like he owned the place.

"I've got a couple of surprises for you," Mr. Calhoun was saying. "In the first place, there are about twice as many seedlings left over as I figured there would be, so the winner gets more than he bargained for." Mose grinned from ear to ear. "In the second place, I'm not awarding the prize to the boy who thinks he's won."

There was dead silence. A startled look wiped the grin clean off Mose Moody's face. Jeb could feel his heart beating double time, as if he'd been running. He caught his breath, waiting for Mr. Calhoun to go on.

"The seedlings go to Jeb Judson."

Jeb didn't move. There must be a mistake. He couldn't have heard what he thought he had.

"Hooray for Jeb!" hollered Little Lije.

Then Mose Moody found his voice. "You cain't do that to me, Callahan Calhoun!" He shook his fist at the boss. "I won them seedlin's fair and square. Sam knows I won 'em. Ever'body here knows I got mine all planted first."

"That's right, Mr. Calhoun," put in Hezzie.

"What makes you think the one who finished first is the winner?" asked Mr. Calhoun.

"You said so and you know hit!" hollered Mose.

"But that wasn't all I said," the boss went on. "I said the one who finished first and *did the best job* would get the seedlings. Jeb did both."

"He never done no such of a thing!" argued Mose. "He never got done till long after me and Hezzie both had finished ourn."

"Jeb came third," said Mr. Calhoun, "with as fine a job of tree planting as I've ever seen. But as far as I'm concerned he was first too, Mose, because neither you nor Hezzie have finished your job yet." While everybody stared, Mr. Calhoun walked over to the last group of trees Mose had planted and pulled up several of the seedlings. "Both you boys will have to replant most of what you did this morning before I'll consider the job done and pay you off accordingly. You've planted too shallow—even if the seedlings lived they'd stand a poor chance of growing to healthy stock. You can come back and finish up in the morning if you count on getting your money before Christmas."

For a second it looked as if Mose might hit Mr. Calhoun. Instead, he rammed his fists into his pockets, glared threateningly at Jeb, and walked away without another word. Hezzie followed.

It didn't take long after that for Foreman Sam to pay off the rest of the boys, and almost before he knew it Jeb was left alone with Little Lije. Everybody else had gone.

"Them's sure a fine crop of seedlin's," said Little Lije. "What you figure on doin' with 'em, Jeb?"

"I'm aimin' to give 'em to Paw for Christmas," he answered. "Mr. Calhoun says I can leave 'em right here till then."

"Well, I'm glad you got 'em, Jeb, instead of Mose," said Little Lije. "He's right riled now account of losin', but he'll git over it. He didn't want 'em nohow, not like me and you did. He don't mean no harm,

67

though, Mose don't. He jest likes to talk big.'"

"He didn't bother me none," declared Jeb, not altogether truthfully.

Little Lije looked like he had something on his mind but he didn't quite know how to say it. "Reckon maybe I better mosey along," he said finally, turning to leave. Then he stopped and looked back at Jeb. "I was jest thinkin'—maybe you could come down to our place, next time Gabe's over that-a-way. We might could go huntin', get us a rabbit or two."

Jeb realized then for the first time that he had made a friend, the only one he'd ever really had, except Dovey. An unfamiliar kind of happiness came over him, and he answered the questioning smile of Little Lije with a grin of his own.

"I'd sure admire to, Lije," he said.

It was still around middle-day, with plenty of time ahead for the long walk home. The two boys started out together, then had to separate when they reached the big road. They said good-by, and Jeb stood watching as Little Lije walked away. He hated for his new friend to go. No telling when he'd have a chance to see him again. Then an idea came to him and he started running, calling as he ran.

"Lije! Lije! Wait a minute."

Little Lije stopped and looked around.

"I jest thought of somethin'," said Jeb, panting a little from the run. "Cain't figure why hit never come to me before. How'd you like to have some of them seedlin's to put out on that land your pa's fixin' to give you?"

Little Lije's face lit up, then darkened again with doubt. "Ain't nothin' I'd rather have," he said slowly. "You know that."

"Well, Mr. Calhoun said there was twice as many left as he'd figured on," said Jeb. "There's aplenty for me 'n' you both."

"How much you want for 'em?" Little Lije wanted to know.

"Shucks, I don't want no pay," said Jeb. "But I'll be needin' help to set 'em out. Figured you might could give me a hand; then you could take the rest of the seedlin's."

Little Lije's eyes lit up again as the doubt went away from his face. "You've jest made yourself a deal, Jeb," he said. "Me 'n' you can get them plants set out in no time, and do you have any left I'd sure admire to take 'em off your hands. I got to be goin' now—see you later."

"So long," said Jeb. He started whistling as he headed for home. He knew now how a man feels when he figures out a way to help a friend. It was a good feeling.

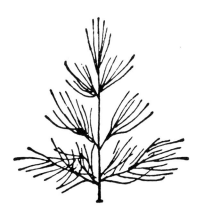

My Gift

BY CHRISTINA ROSSETTI

Illustrated by Frank Murphy

What can I give Him
Poor as I am;
If I were a shepherd,
I would give Him a lamb.
If I were a wise man,
I would do my part.
But what can I give Him?
I will give my heart.

Maggie Rose's Christmas Birthday

BY RUTH SAWYER

Illustrated by Meg Wohlberg

Maggie Rose was born on Christmas Eve, and she wanted
something special for her ninth birthday. She wanted her
family, the Bunkers, to *give* a party for all their
neighbors instead of taking gifts of food and clothing
and many other things as they usually did. Maggie Rose
worked and saved, but her money was stolen. It was then
that Tim and Liz, her parents, and her big brothers
Fuss and Feathers, and her little brother and sisters all
joined in to work and help make Maggie Rose's dream
come true. Her summertime friends, the Admiral and Jeremy,
and her teacher-friend, Myra Moon, and everybody in
the little Maine town where Maggie Rose lived helped, too.
Here is the joyous and exciting story of Maggie Rose
and her Christmas-birthday party.

S NOW CAME. The winter sky grew brittle and colors such as
summer never gave were scattered from horizon to horizon. The
water of the bay gave back the colors, until Maggie Rose said it was
just like being done up in Christmas wrappings. The days "before"
flew; every one held its own surprise. Bob, the best carpenter, along
with Joe, the next best, arrived early one morning and said they had
come to put in new glass in the windows—so the house would keep
warm against a cold, long winter. Saturday, neighbors came, to put
in a sturdy doorsill, to fix a cupboard in the kitchen for dishes. All
the nails were pulled out of the walls and a place was fixed in the
empty front room to hang all Bunker clothes.

Myra Moon came with some muslin curtains, used but fresh-
laundered and ruffled; and Bob put up the rods while she measured
and cut them off the right length. Everybody turned to and cleaned
windows and floors, polished the Clarion Range, put gay shelf paper

on the corner shelves. By nightfall it was another kitchen; and Maggie Rose sat in it, waiting for Tim and Liz to come home, and for the baby, thinking — knowing — that already her birthday Christmas celebration had begun. "It's a nice kitchen. It's enough for anyone on the whole Point. The minute the cradle's back in its place, seems like I couldn't ask for another thing."

But others came to add more to her delight. Neighbors brought chairs they did not really need, braided scatter rugs to cover the bareness of the floor. The postmaster came up with a huge basket of dishes.

"We don't need these. Better put them away in that new cupboard. They'll come in handy for the party Monday night."

"Thank you—oh, thank you. The kitchen is so full of surprises and pretty things—seems like it would burst; or we Bunkers would." By the time everyone had come home Maggie Rose had a good dinner started; but she had taken long, troubled looks at the kitchen walls, with the paper torn off in spots and the plaster falling. Suddenly she had an idea. It was wonderful—out of this world—as the Admiral's granddaughter would say. But the idea must keep. She must hold on to it until every Bunker had eaten, and rested, and was as full of contentment as she was.

It was like being surprised twice over to watch the face of each as he opened the door, stepped inside, and took one look. "Looks like we had us a kitchen bee," said Tim. . . . "Pretty—so pretty," said Liz, choking with the sudden wonder of it. The children whooped and danced; while the baby, still in Tim's arms, laughed and laughed until hiccoughs came. Such a merry time; and more money to put in the alligator bag. As always, Maggie Rose counted it, stuffed it thankfully inside and said: "That's to begin the New

Year on. It might—it might almost pay for a sink and a pump and a pipe to run into the kitchen. Likely all of us are as tired of lugging water as we are of eating canned beans."

"Likely we are," said Tim. And he said it as if he meant it.

The little girls washed up. With everything put away and tidy, to match the wonderful kitchen, Maggie Rose sat down in one of the new-given chairs and folded her hands very tight on her lap. She sat so straight and stiff that Tim eyed her with a mixture of trouble and curiosity. "What's stirrin' you up now, Maggie Rose?"

"I'm just thinking. Tomorrow's Sunday. First we'll all go to Chapel. They always count on us Bunkers to swell the carols. After that— there's just one thing more I'd like to ask. While mumma and me are baking, you—puppa—and the boys could cut balsam boughs —lots of them—and line the walls, floor to ceiling. It would cover over the awful places; and make us so Christmasy and sweet-smell- ing. We could have a spruce tree, whole, for the corner, there. And when we hang the lanterns and fix the snow-garlands and everything, it will look the prettiest kitchen this side of heaven."

Fuss started to grumble: "Aw—Maggie Rose—have a heart— we've been working. . . ."

Gently Tim shut him up. "The princess is right. Seems like we should take it up where the neighbors left off—show what we Bunkers can do. We'll give them the surprise of their lives."

So it was settled.

The eight walking Bunkers, well clad from the clothes heap, with the baby snugly wrapped in a blanket and carried proudly by Tim, made what one might call "the grand entrance" that Christmas Sunday. They filled the front of the Chapel. Maggie Rose unbundled the baby that all might see the little blue flannel dress she wore and the blue ribbon tied about her hair, which was beginning to curl.

Everyone came. Someone had brought sprigs of pine and spruce to put here and there; on the reading desk there was a fine bunch of red berries with more green. To Maggie Rose, Preacher Thomas seemed particularly holy. The carols chosen were their favorites. Never had those Bunkers sung with more spirit and sweetness. When the plate was passed, everyone, even the baby, had something to put in. And just before the benediction Preacher Thomas said: "I see we have our family of singers here today. I think if we asked them to sing 'Holy Night' just before the benediction they would be glad to. Then, I think we would go our ways feeling we had attended a very special Christmas service."

For the rest of the day Bunker shoulders were bent to work. Maggie Rose and her mother stirred up and baked every variety of cake-mix that George had in the store: white and spiced, devil's food and cup cakes. The older boys chopped boughs; Bugs dragged them in; and Tim nailed them along the lengths of the pine uprights. Before more than one wall was covered, all began to feel the enchantment that was taking place before their eyes. "Deck the halls with boughs of holly," sang Maggie Rose. "Only our halls are being decked with balsam—and I don't believe holly could be nicer."

Myra Moon came over in the early dusk and stood fairly speechless at what she saw. "I came over to ice the cakes for you; but you'll have to wait till I get my breath again."

She had brought her best lace tablecloth for the party table; and spoons and forks and extra cups. She did a splendid job frosting the cakes—fluffy frosting, orange icing, chocolate spread. When the cakes were done, they looked magnificent.

The tree was put up last; and then everyone except the baby had the fun of decorating. The lanterns Jeremy had made, with the Admiral's help, not only hung from the tree but clear around the room, making a row halfway down the balsam walls. Then came the snow-garlands. Tim and Maggie Rose hung them; these took gentle hands, being so fragile. There seemed to be miles of garlands, enough for walls and tree; and the smaller fry hung the silvered cones and the few colored balls Maggie Rose had bought. Here a silver one, there a red one.

It was unbelievably lovely when everything was finished. Myra looked at Maggie Rose. "To me it looks like a dream come true."

Tim said: "Never seen anything like it before. I'd call it plain handsome."

It was Maggie Rose who spoke last: "It's a place fitten to celebrate a birthday Christmas. And I'm thinking of His."

Monday broke overcast. By noon snow was falling. It would be a white Christmas, the first in three years. Neighbors arrived early with cookies they had insisted on baking. Some were stars, and those delighted Maggie Rose. The rural delivery man stopped. The boys watched from the window and reported in loud voices: "He's leaving slathers of mail. Packages. Looks like the box is crammed full." They pelted out to bring it in, without benefit of coat or scarf, or even sweater. One package was addressed to "Miss Margaret Rose Bunker." In the corner it said: "From Jeremy Peters." And underneath: "To be opened *before* Christmas."

"Open it, open it!" They were all crowding around her, begging. But it seemed too precious to open. To have a present from Jeremy! She just wanted to hold it tight and read over and over what was written on the outside of the box. "Better open it," said Tim. "Then look at your cards. Seems like everyone from the Point has sent you one."

"Let's all take turns with the cards. Then I'll open Jeremy's." So in turn each card was taken from its envelope and the greeting read, along with the sender's name. There was a second package—this from the Admiral—and Maggie Rose opened this first. Inside were four tin candlesticks, made of shining tin angels, each holding a red candle. The card inside said: "For Maggie Rose with my love. To put in the windows for the birthday Christmas."

But she still waited, putting off the moment when she should open and unwrap Jeremy's present. The urging around her grew too loud, too insistent. Feathers cut the twine with his knife. With the outer wrappings off, there showed the gayest inside wrapping, white with Christmas trees all over it, tied with red and tinsel ribbon. The card tied to it said: "For Maggie Rose—with tinkling bells. From Jeremy."

"What does he mean 'with tinkling bells'?" asked Fuss.

"Open and see. Quick!" This from Vi.

What was inside looked very shiny—shiny as gold, and very complicated. There were several small packages; and a picture with printing, and the words at the top read: "Christmas Chimes." Here again were the figures of three angels, and a wheel, and what looked like different sized gongs, three of them. There was a shaftlike thing with a point. And a star to fit on the top. Last of all there were three candles. "It's something to put together," said Fuss—the one who was cleverest with his hands. He gathered up everything, with the picture, and took them to the table. There he set to work. On a small round tray he fitted the angels. From that point on he read directions and put things together until everything including the candles were in their right places. "It says here to light the candles and the heat they send up will turn the wheel and ring the chimes. All right to light them, Maggie Rose?"

The little girl was too speechless to do anything but nod her head. For minutes after the candles were lighted everyone waited for something to happen. Nothing did. Had it been put together wrong? Had they been cheated? "The old thing won't work," said Feathers.

It was at that moment that the wheel began to turn. Very slowly

at first, then faster and faster. From the wheel hung little metal clappers. These struck against the gongs. They made a slow, low tinkle at first, that grew more distinct, until suddenly the sound of sweet chimes filled the room. No one spoke. No one wanted to do anything but listen and marvel. It was Maggie Rose who broke the spell. "It's a sort of praising God and singing. Now let's blow out the candles and keep them to light again tonight when everyone is here."

It was Myra Moon who came at dusk Christmas Eve, the bearer of cookies and a box so big it hardly fitted under one arm. "I thought maybe you'd like some help setting up the table. Brought extra candles in case." Then she put the box into Maggie Rose's arms and said: "Good plan to open it now. See if the dresses fit."

The box held three little dresses, red woolen, and three different sizes. It was only then that Maggie Rose realized those Bunkers were having a party and had nothing to dress up in. Maybe this was the time for Liz to open her new dress, and Tim and the boys to put on their new flannel shirts. She skipped into the cold front room, hunted through the packages and came back with the right things. Myra stood by and admired. The dress for Liz was pretty, a dark brown with a full skirt and pretty buttons. The flannel shirts fitted, and

they were gay plaids. Tim chuckled his delight; and the boys said: "Boy, oh, boy!" Each little girl held her dress up under her chin. They looked red as Christmas berries, and every dress was the right length, with room for growing.

While the Bunkers changed, Myra set up the table, spread the lace cloth, put red candles at each end; set forth the plates of cookies and cakes. There was barely room for stacking cups and the paper napkins and plates Maggie Rose had bought in Bangor.

A few moments later the family were back, party dressed, and Maggie Rose spoke what was in her mind: "We look nice. We look like other folks belonging on the Point." She looked across the room to Myra and gave her an impish grin. "Remember what you said when I came to tell you first of anybody about the birthday Christmas? You said then—we didn't need to ask the Queen to be our cousin. Well—that's what I'm thinking this minute."

Myra stayed for supper—a light one—and they were all proud to have her. Everyone had a hand at doing the last-minute things: to wash up; to light the candles the Admiral had sent and put them in the windows; to set the kettles, one borrowed, to boiling, and build up the fire; to have the big coffee-maker from the Community House ready to fill, and set the pot of cocoa to the back of the stove. Last of all to take down and light each lantern, and the candles of the Christmas chimes.

The room was full of warmth, of welcome, and of the soft tinkling of bells, as feet, many feet, sounded on the road outside. Maggie Rose thought with a quick upsurge of gladness: This year I'm not looking from outside into other people's houses. This year I'm looking from the inside! It was all too big and wonderful to put into mere words. Instead she listened to the feet coming nearer, coming to their house, the house of "those Bunkers"!

Lots of cold air came in with every group of guests. Everyone had to stand breathlessly in the doorway, taking in the walls, the tree, the lighted lanterns, the tinkling chimes. No one had ever seen a Christmas like this; no one had ever imagined lining walls with boughs or making snow-garlands with old strips of tissue paper.

It was the gayest party. Even the baby stayed awake to gurgle her delight. Every time a fresh batch of neighbors arrived Maggie Rose was sure there would not be room, but there always was. George brought some folding chairs and set them up when needed. Children scrooched on the floor. It was after everybody had come that Maggie Rose suddenly remembered the huge bag full of peppermint candy canes she had bought. "Clean forgot them," she explained as she passed them out. "This celebration has been so packed full I'd have forgotten my own head if it hadn't been firm-fastened on."

That brought laughter. Soon the room was filled with the smell of making coffee. There was plenty for everyone; and that in itself was almost a miracle to those Bunkers, who had so often gone hungry.

Cups were filled, twice over. There was cake for everyone to have two pieces; and cookies—as many as anyone could eat. Never had food been offered and shared with such generous out-giving. Neighbors who said they had "just dropped in for a moment" stayed until midnight.

Preacher Thomas drove all the way from the next township, bringing his wife and a present for Maggie Rose. The present was large and heavy and sharp-cornered. He put it into Maggie Rose's arms saying: "It belonged to my family. I thought there wasn't anyone who would treasure it more."

The little girl did not have to be told what it was. Carefully she put it down under the tree, asking the children packed around it to move. From that moment Maggie Rose's eyes shone like stars. She could only make sounds like a small chirping bird when people spoke to her. In time children fell asleep, heads on laps nearest them. Before the midnight hour came, everyone, as if by general accord, broke into singing: "It came upon a midnight clear." The carol filled the room; and singing, Maggie Rose thought: It's come. For Him, just born; and for me, nine years old.

It was right and fitting to finish with "Oh, Little Town of Bethlehem." Children were awakened softly to it, coats and mufflers were put on to music from every throat. Fathers shouldering their sons and daughters went out into the night, still singing; mothers and grandmothers followed with nods, sometimes breaking into "Merry Christmas," only to go back to their caroling:

"How silently, how silently the wond'rous gift is given!"

Those Bunkers stood in the open doorway, Maggie Rose pressed hard against Tim's knees, singing the last of the carol into the night. Strangely no sound of hurrying feet, no sound of clamoring voices came back to them. Tim looked over her head and said: "Stars are out, Maggie Rose, same as when you were born."

They went inside and blew out all the candles. Only the old china lamp on the table gave any light. For a moment everyone milled about the kitchen, too tired to stay up much longer, too happy and full of the celebration to go to bed. Maggie Rose settled the matter for them.

"I want everyone to sit down. Sit close around the lamp. The birthday Christmas isn't over yet." She went to the tree and got the present Preacher Thomas had brought. With adoring fingers she took off the wrappings and showed it. "The Holy Book! I knew it was. See—just like the one in Chapel, and for our very own. Now we have a book, belonging to us—like other folks. There isn't another book in the whole world like it. It's got *gold letters* on it, saying HOLY BIBLE. It's got gold edges to it." She opened it, turning to the old

engraving of the Ascension. "It has pictures. It has reading—all the words every one of the preachers have read are here, inside, and we can read them."

A great stillness filled the room. The smaller of the children, Connie and Bugs, had climbed into their parents' laps. The baby had long ago gone to sleep. Strangely enough although everyone knew there were presents waiting in the empty front room, waiting to be brought to the kitchen to be unwrapped and exclaimed over, not one of those Bunkers was thinking of them now.

They were waiting for Maggie Rose to find what she was looking for, turning the pages slowly in that Holy Book she knew so well—and yet did not know at all. She stood very straight, very quietly, beside the table, one finger pointing to the page. Then she looked over her shoulder and smiled at all her family. She said in a small hushed voice: "It's the story, the holy story. Listen:

"And there were in the same country shepherds abiding in the field, keeping watch over their flock by night. And, lo, the angel of the Lord came upon them, and the glory of the Lord shone round about them; and they were sore afraid. And the angel said unto them Fear not: for, behold, I bring you tidings of great joy. . . ."

Barter

BY SARA TEASDALE

Illustrated by Meg Wohlberg

Life has loveliness to sell,
  All beautiful and splendid things,
Blue waves whitened on a cliff,
  Soaring fire that sways and sings.
And children's faces looking up
Holding wonder like a cup.

Life has loveliness to sell,
  Music like a curve of gold,
Scent of pine trees in the rain,
  Eyes that love you, arms that hold,
And for your spirit's delight,
Holy thoughts that star the night.

Spend all you have for loveliness,
  Buy it and never count the cost;
For one white singing hour of peace
  Count many a year of strife well lost,
And for a breath of ecstasy
Give all you have been, or could be.

Wise

BY AILEEN FISHER

Illustrated by Wesley Dennis

Whoever planned
the world was wise
to think of land
and seas, and skies.

To plan a sun
and moon that could
be made to run
the way they should.

But how did He
have time for all
the things we see
that are so small—

Like flowers in parks
and flakes of snow
and little sparks
the fireflies show?

The Little Foxes

BY VIRGINIA SORENSEN

Illustrated by Wesley Dennis

Miracles do happen. Ten-year-old Marly discovered that
when she came to live on Maple Hill. Father had been
ill. Now he was growing strong and happy again. That
was one kind of miracle. Other kinds of miracles
were happening, too. One day Marly and her brother Joe
went exploring. This is the story of what happened then.

IT WAS THE VERY LAST FRIDAY before the very last week of
school. As they drove up the hill Mother always called "the great
slippery" because of that first time they were stuck on it, Joe suddenly said something wonderful to Marly. "You know, there's the
queerest place up this side of the sugarbush. Moss all over on great
big bumps. I'll show it to you tomorrow, if you want."

She held her breath. Had he explored and explored until now he
had started to want to show somebody?

"We called those bump-things hummocks," Mother said.

"Some are ant-towns," Joe said. "The little ones." He smiled at
Marly. "I'll show you tomorrow."

She could tell he had something very special on his mind. "Shall
I fix a lunch?" she asked. He liked it when she fixed a lunch if it
didn't slow them up too much getting started. "I can get up real
early and fix it."

"That'll be swell," he said.

So at last, she thought, the time had come. Now she could go anywhere and be as safe as could be. Even if there were cows, with
Joe she wouldn't need to be one bit afraid. She was awake so early

85

the next morning that the birds had hardly beat her to it. As she hurried with the sandwiches and cookies and fruit, she kept humming inside, like a cat.

Joe was surprised to find her all ready when he came down—and how pleased! There she was, waiting on the back step with two neat sacks beside her, one for herself and one for him, only his exactly twice as big.

Joe explained some things on the way up the road. Maple Mountain was strange, Mr. Chris said, because it had swamps and bogs right up in its highest places. The humpy-bumpy meadows on top were part of its queerness too. Joe and Marly went from one hump to the other, opened some to watch ants, and looked at the queer moss and starry little plants on others. Joe had his magnifying glass, and they gazed into the strangest worlds, with funny little bugs tumbling around in the moss like animals in a jungle.

They went on to a little valley, then, and followed a brook that made one huge curve after another, doubling itself over like a coiled rope.

Joe said the curves were "meanders," and he showed her rocks in the stream bed that were full of ancient shells. They'd been left there ages ago when the ocean was practically everywhere. There were scrapings on the big stones and perfectly round stones that Joe said were shaped by huge slides of ice that were in that very spot about a million years ago—or maybe a billion. Marly couldn't think what the difference might be with those numbers, only that one was lots bigger than the other.

She felt proud of all Joe knew. Maybe Mr. Chris knew about flowers and birds and things, but Joe was the one who knew about bugs and the queer plants that grew on stumps and fallen trees. They had nice names, too. For instance, there were funny things like little plugged-up funnels, some gray called pixie-cups and some bright red called British soldiers. And there were odd little shelves that looked like they'd been made for fairies to sit on. Only Joe said they were just wood rot. On old logs there were tall black things called deadman's-fingers. And one funny toadstool was bright yellow, called a jack-o-lantern, that Joe said really gave light at night.

86

"Joe, you know more things than Mr. Chris," Marly said.

To her surprise he said, "Oh, no, I don't! Nobody knows more than Chris. Who do you think told me most of that stuff? We came out here last week, and Chris showed me some things I wanted to show you. In the fall around here there are mushrooms all over, if you know where to find 'em. One of Mr. Chris's hired men, before Fritz, used to gather quarts and quarts and sell 'em to an Italian in town and make a mint of money every fall."

She hardly heard the last of it. "Joe," she said, "Mr. Chris didn't climb clear up this hill, did he? Why, if Chrissie heard about that—"

Joe went red. He pretended not to hear what she was saying but leaned over and then knelt right down on the ground. "Look there, at that striped beetle. Blister beetle, that's who! When we get to a pool I found, I'll show you some diving beetles too. You ever see a whirligig?"

"Joe—did he?" she asked. "Because he shouldn't. Chrissie told me to look out for him and not let him climb even the littlest hill. And this one—" She looked behind them at the steep path.

"You know, the other day I saw a huge bumblebee caught in a lady-slipper," Joe said. "Couldn't get out to save him. I could hear him a block off, roaring—"

Marly interrupted. It wasn't because she wasn't interested in that bumblebee, but Joe had to know about taking care of Mr. Chris if he didn't know it already. "Joe, you and Chris were supposed to go into town that day in the car."

He stood up suddenly and turned to her. "I guess you'll go right and tell!" he said. "Just like a girl, can't keep anything to herself! Sure we went to town. We talked with that man in the restaurant, see. He buys all his syrup from Mr. Chris and says it's the best syrup in the world. He buys all his apple juice from Mr. Chris, too. And he says he used to buy chestnuts—but that's been years and years. After, Mr. Chris and I came up here, and he showed me those old chestnut snags—see, along there? There used to be so many you could get a half bushel of chestnuts in an hour."

"Joe, Mr. Chris didn't walk clear up here, *did* he?" Marly asked.

"You shouldn't *ever* let him, Chrissie said. She told me we've got to help, because when he gets interested in showing people things, he just forgets."

"Okay, okay. We walked real slow. And he told me how this country used to look. Lots more forest than now. Between diseases like the one that killed all the chestnuts, and then people timbering the land, he says almost all the virgin forest is gone now."

Marly stood still. As if what Joe said had started the sound, she suddenly began to hear the whine of a saw. From Mr. Chris's place? "Joe, Mr. Chris isn't cutting down trees, is he? Just for money? He told me he never would."

"Of course he's not." He looked disgusted that she should even ask. "But I want to watch them cutting that tree. It's an old maple," he said.

As they walked, the whining of the saw grew louder and louder until it seemed to make huge circles of sound through the woods. They made a big circle and came finally to the sugarbush.

Mr. Chris was there with Fritz and a strange man with an electric saw. The old tree at which the saw was working was dead except one great branch that stood green among the masses of brown boughs. It was over a yard thick and was giving the saw a very hard time of it.

Mr. Chris waved to Marly and Joe as they came. When he talked, he had to shout over the ugly whining of the saw. "A grand old tree," he said. "A good sugar tree, for years and years. I've tapped it every season until this last one, for at least thirty years. We used to boil the sap right over there—had a long oven and one big pan. You can even see the old stones where the oven was."

Joe and Marly stood watching. They didn't try to talk, and Mr. Chris didn't say any more, either, for a while. The saw's humming was almost a scream as it got near the center of the trunk. Mr. Chris leaned close to Marly's ear. "When she falls, we'll count the rings and see just how old she is," he said.

A red squirrel began scolding from another tree. Mr. Chris looked up and shook his fist, laughing. "It's all right, old fellow," he called. "We're leaving you your butternut tree. But this old maple is going to come home with us and keep us warm this winter."

The squirrel sat looking at him, its paws folded in front as if it might be saying its prayers. Then the great maple began to crack and groan, and the squirrel turned and vanished into a hole. Fritz shouted, "Watch out! She's coming down!"

Like a giant, the great tree fell. Its immense dead limbs struck the ground first and broke, crashing, and it sagged and roared and seemed to fight with the air. For a minute it lay trembling all over. Then it was still.

Marly wanted to cry. But Joe laughed and yelled, "Hurrah! Boy, oh boy!" and before the tree had really settled down, he was into the branches. And then he was counting the rings. That tree had been growing for over a hundred years.

It was dusk as they started for home. Now that the saw had ceased to whine, the silence seemed immense and wonderful. They could hear the rustling of the trees that still stood up straight into the air.

Suddenly, just as they came to the hummocky place, Joe clutched Marly's arm. And then, without warning, he laid his hand hard across her mouth, whispering, "Sssssh!"

It was lucky he saw it first or she might have yelled the way she did when she saw the deer. Joe whispered, "Look!"

Up on one of those bumpy hummocks, just standing with its huge bushy tail straight out behind, was a red fox. It stood looking down the hill, one paw lifted like a puppy paying attention to everything. Then it leaped suddenly to another hummock and stood there, looking. The sun was down, and a weird light was over everything, so the fox seemed to have a shine all over.

Marly and Joe didn't move. Neither did the fox. Finally, then, without a sound, looking like a colored shadow, the fox slipped from the hummock and was gone. It disappeared into the ravine, by the brook.

"I'll bet she's got a den around here," Joe said. His voice was low, and when he walked, he walked easy in a certain way he knew, the way he had learned Indians walked. Marly couldn't hear him past ten yards. She wanted to call, "Don't go out of sight, Joe," because dark was starting and there was that strange light, rather eerie, as night fell over Maple Mountain. But she didn't call. She didn't make a sound.

In a minute she was glad she didn't. Joe came slipping back out of the shadow, beckoning.

"Ssssh! And don't fall over anything!" he said.

"Joe, what is it?"

"Sssssh . . ."

At one place the hill went suddenly down, rocky and steep. At the top Joe took hold of her arm hard, and then he pointed with his other hand.

In the dusk were five little foxes, playing together. They tumbled about like puppies. They chased each other. They made little growly sounds, pretending to fight. They were all red, except for their black pointed noses and their sharp black ears, and each one had a white tip on its long red tail.

Joe and Marly watched until they couldn't see a thing but the white tips on the tails. Then these too vanished.

Joe led Marly toward home, over the hummocks, holding her by the hand. She had never loved him so much in all her life. "Joe, if it hadn't been for you, I'd never have seen anything like that. Not *ever*," she said.

"Why not? I see things all the time," he said. But she could tell he was pleased that she had said it.

The Chrises and Fritz were at the house when they got back. As soon as Marly got into the door and saw them, she cried, "Guess what we saw, Joe and me, up by the high pasture. Some *fox* . . ." And then she said, suddenly, "Ouch!" because Joe had given her a good big pinch.

He hadn't done it soon enough. She already had the word out of her mouth.

Fritz leaned forward in his chair. "Foxes, huh? So that's where they are!" He turned to Mr. Chris. "I knew they were around close somewhere, didn't I, Chris? I can go in the morning. Maybe if I go before light, I can grab the whole bunch."

Grab them? Marly felt her eyes go wide. "Fritz, you don't mean you want to catch those little foxes, do you?" she said. "Why, this one has five babies, the cutest little puppies—"

She saw Joe's look. Oh, she never never knew when to keep her mouth shut! That's what his look said to her, as plain as day.

"Five little ones, huh? No wonder she's been busy," Mr. Chris said. "How many chickens does that take every day? Every day for a solid week that she-devil has been at my chickens. We put the flock in the coop last night, and she got in under the wall. Or her mate it was. If they aren't the cleverest—"

"And that dog, Tony, doesn't even notice any more," Chrissie said. "I tell Chris he's too old for a watchdog now. He sleeps like a stone."

Marly's mouth felt dry. "What are you going to do?" she asked. She didn't dare even look at Joe.

A little silence fell. Everybody suddenly remembered Marly and those mice.

"Well," Mr. Chris said, and gave a queer little cough, "to tell you the truth, Marly, this country is overrun with foxes the past few years." He turned back to Fritz and Daddy as if he'd rather not talk to her about it any more. "There's a good big bounty on them now, and if you want to fix the pelts up, you can get more." Then he looked straight at Joe. "You show Fritz the place in the morning, Joe. Maybe you can get a shot or so yourself."

Was this Mr. Chris? Marly gazed at him.

"Tell you what, we'll split the bounty, Joe, no matter who gets 'em," Fritz said. He was a good shot, Marly knew; she'd heard them tell about how many rabbits and pheasants and squirrels Fritz got in hunting season.

"Okay," Joe said.

Marly turned to him in unbelief. After seeing those little foxes playing as the sun went down! "Joe, you wouldn't!" she said.

"Those things eat mice, too," Mr. Chris said hastily. "Marly, they eat hundreds and hundreds of mice. If I just had livestock and grain or even orchards, I'd say the more foxes the better. But chickens—"

Marly couldn't manage another word or stand to hear one. Everybody was agreeing, and she knew there wasn't any use. If even *Joe* —after what he had seen! Suddenly the words of the song Daddy sang sometimes came back to her. Not the song about the fox coming for the big black duck, heavens no! But the one about the cruel hunters in their red coats and the nice boy who felt sorry for the fox and refused to tell them which way it had gone. Had Joe forgotten?

When the Chrises and Fritz went away, Fritz called back to Joe that he'd be calling by real early, maybe about five o'clock. Joe went right up to bed, then, without a word, and Marly felt herself go cold all over. She reached for Daddy's arm as he started for the stairs. "Daddy—about the foxes—"

"Marly, please," Mother said. "There's no earthly use of your worrying about things like that. You've got to learn."

"I was only going to ask Daddy to sing tonight," Marly said. "Those foxes made me think about the fox songs."

Daddy and Mother looked at each other.

"First the one about the fox stealing the goose," Marly said to get them off the track of what she meant to do. Then, she thought, if Daddy would sing the one about the hunters and the wonderful kind boy who wouldn't tell them where the fox went, Joe would understand what she was going to say when she went upstairs. He couldn't help but understand, after that song.

"Well, all right. Just those two, then," Daddy said. "You know, 93

Lee, I'm getting so I can do the hunting song pretty well again."

And he really could. The first verse about the hunters coming and the horns blowing and the scarlet coats went really fast. Marly opened the door to the stairs so Joe would be sure to hear.

> " 'Say there, youngster,' the huntsmen cry,
> 'Say, have you seen the fox go by?
> Galloping, galloping, galloping, galloping,
> Galloping, galloping over the hill?' "

"Now," Marly thought, and opened the door a little wider. This was the verse for Joe to hear.

> "But would I be telling them? No, not I!
> That I saw the fox go wearily by?
> Wearily panting, worn and spent,
> Would I be telling the way he went,
> Galloping . . . galloping . . . galloping . . ."

Daddy was wonderful, the way he made the words sound slow and tired as if the poor fox was ready to drop. Then suddenly he shouted the last two words: *No! Not I!*"

It made Marly's hair wiggle every time she heard it, it was so wonderful. But especially tonight. She kissed Daddy good night more fervently than ever before and went upstairs, closing the door after her. But Joe's door was closed, and his light was out.

So he didn't want to talk about it.

But she did. She had to. She opened his door just a crack and whispered, "Joe . . ."

No sound.

"*Joe*," she said.

Suddenly he spoke. He wasn't in bed at all. He was sitting in the dark by the window. "Just shut up for a while," he said in a low voice. "Can you? I've got to figure out what we can do. If I went over and threw rocks and tramped all over there where the den is . . . See, if I could just scare them out of there before Fritz can get there . . ."

"Oh, Joe, of course you can!" she said. And then, excitedly, "Tonight? Joe, way over to the hill tonight?"

His voice sounded disgusted. "I can't very well wait until morning this time, can I? If Fritz ever heard of me doing a thing like that, he'd think I was crazy. Why, there are seven of 'em right there. Four dollars' bounty apiece! That's a lot of money!" She felt his eyes through the dark. "If you just didn't have to tell everything you know! Sometimes I think it's better never to tell you anything—or show you anything."

"Joe, I'm so sorry. Honest, I'll never, never tell anything again. Why, I just thought Mr. Chris and Chrissie and Fritz would love those little foxes." She looked beyond Joe, out of the window. It was deep-dark and scary, and she shivered. "Joe, it'll be horrible to go clear over there past all those bumpy places and everything in the dark."

"If I took a light and then just shot at the ground near the den," he said, thinking aloud, his voice very low. "I guess you could go along and hold the light, couldn't you? Just so we get 'em out of there."

"Joe—you mean I can go?" She felt a glow everywhere, a happiness that was like suddenly running out of the cold into a warm, bright house. She had put the foxes in danger, but now she could go out into the night and help make them safe again.

"The trouble is maybe they'll fight. I don't know. Look what it says in my *Field Book*." She closed the door, and he turned his light on and showed her the place. "Look—'Male feeds female and young, and leads enemies away from den at risk of his life.'"

"We're not enemies," she said. "It's Fritz he should lead away."

"Too bad Father Fox doesn't know that, now isn't it?" Joe asked. "You say the silliest things I ever heard of. But it's not a question of leading Fritz away—he knows where the den is now."

"If only I hadn't mentioned it!" she cried.

"Well, that's spilled milk now. You didn't know." He sat staring at the book as if it might give him an idea. "Maybe if we built a little fire by one door we could smoke 'em out the other, like bees," he said. "They always have a front door and a back door."

She was enchanted. "Joe, how clever—a front door and a back door—"

"Now just act like you're going to bed," he told her. "But put on 95 some warm socks and things. We'll go as soon as Dad and Mother are asleep."

What ages it seemed before Daddy and Mother came upstairs, before they were finally finished in the bathroom and had climbed into bed, before Daddy finally began to snore! Marly heard Joe's door open. She was so excited she could hardly breathe, and a funny little pain started at the back of her neck. Moving as silently as possible, she followed Joe's shadow down the stairs. He was getting the flashlights out of the drawer. Then he got a pocketful of matches and a rag and the can of kerosene.

Goodness, but that road was dark! Joe led the way, only flashing a light once in a while and then very briefly. They passed Chris's house, all dark, and went on to the field and the pasture. How wide and high the night was! Marly had never seen it look so huge. She looked up with the biggest, highest feeling she'd ever had in all her life as they started up the hill. If it hadn't been for Joe walking close ahead, she knew she'd have been scared enough to die in her tracks. Shadows hung over the road and slipped around the trees and stones when Joe flashed the light.

At the top of the slope where the den was, Joe stood still and waited for a long time. Was he afraid? Marly was scared to think he might be, because if *Joe* was scared . . . Well, that meant it was really dangerous. But he wasn't scared. He was only planning what to do. After a while he spoke quite loud, and she jumped. She had expected he would whisper. "Look, Marly, you shine both flashlights into the hole, see, when I find it. I'll fix this rag, and then we'll light it and stuff it in and run. See?"

"Where'll we run?"

"Back up here. Then we can watch and see what they do."

That was exactly what they did. Joe made a big noise going down the slope, he let rocks roll under him and everything. The sooner the foxes were scared now, the better, of course. They had come to scare foxes.

"Here's the den," he said. It was a real big hole, with grass over the top like a huge eyebrow so nobody would ever have seen it from above. Marly's hands shook so her lights went wobble-wobble.

The rag flared at once, the minute Joe struck the first match, and Joe tossed it in.

And then they ran, stumbling and slipping as they climbed.

They didn't have long to wait. Out of the other door came a long slim shape, and another, and another smaller, and then a whole quick row of them. The flame showed them as plain as plain, and besides Joe suddenly turned a flashlight full onto them. There was a flashing of eyes. And that was all. The rag died down and went out, and there wasn't a sound.

They waited. Far off, a dog barked. Or was it a dog? "I'm not sure the father was here, even," Joe said. "I only saw one big one. Maybe he'd gone off to hunt, and she's calling him."

Once more they heard the barking. It sounded far off. "If that's her barking, she's gone a long way already," Joe said. "I don't think they'll come back here. But in case they do, we'd better put some rocks and things in the doors. Are you too tired?"

"No, I'm not tired at all." It was true. She was too excited to be tired. She worked right beside him, and they put lots of rocks in both the doors.

"Well, I guess that's all we can do," Joe said.

Now that it was over, Marly was so tired she could hardly walk, but she didn't say so. When they got home, they didn't make a sound. Except right at her door Joe suddenly took her arm and squeezed it hard and whispered, "Now keep your mouth shut about this, see? Not a word!"

"Not a word," she said.

"Honest?"

"Honest, Joe. Cross my heart."

That was the last she knew until she heard Fritz give a little honk at dawn. He went everywhere in the truck because he had so much to do from one end of the farm to the other. Joe went down the stairs, and Marly watched from the window. Joe had his gun. She lay shivering so hard she thought she'd be better up. So she went downstairs and built a fire that really burned. She even mixed biscuits.

"Well, look who's up already!" Daddy said. He went outside to listen, and came back and asked, "Have you heard any shots yet, Marly?"

"No," she said.

"And I knew you were listening." He patted her hand. He thought he understood, she thought, but this time he was all wrong. He didn't know *half.* And she would never tell, either, in this world or another.

They didn't ever hear any shooting. Not that morning! Soon they heard the truck instead. Joe got out at the gate and waved his gun to say good-by as Fritz drove away. Marly's heart was beating fast when Joe appeared at the door. She gave him one look—and he winked.

"Funniest thing," he said. "We went right to that place, and there wasn't a sign of a fox. Den's all full of stuff. Fritz said he never saw anything like it before."

Marly ran to look at the biscuits. They were done, huge and brown. She felt as if she would burst clear out of her skin with joy, so she began to sing. "*Galloping . . . galloping . . . galloping . . .*" Her voice cracked when she sang "*No, not I!*" because it was on a note too high for her. But she didn't care.

"I wonder—" Daddy said.

But he didn't say what he wondered, and nobody answered.

The Missing Dollar

BY JERROLD BEIM

Illustrated by Gregory Orloff

Ten-year-old Jeff wore glasses and was shy. When his
father got a new job, managing a grocery store, and the
family moved to Watertown, Jeff found it hard to make
new friends. His older brother, Donnie, was different.
He had a lot of friends, and he didn't understand
Jeff's shyness. Often he teased Jeff by calling him
girls' names. Then one day Donnie got into trouble.
It was Jeff who found the way to help and to prove to
Donnie that brothers should be good friends, too.

THE WEATHER turned colder. Jeff didn't like it because he
couldn't always go outside to play. Sometimes he had to stay upstairs in the apartment with Donnie.

"Mary—Bessie—Elizabeth—Jane—" Donnie would tease whenever
he couldn't get his own way with Jeff. It still made Jeff furious and
he didn't know how to get back at Donnie.

"Just say, 'Sticks and bones will break my bones but names will
never hurt me,'" Mom once advised Jeff.

It didn't work. Donnie just laughed when he said that. Besides,
names did hurt him. They hurt inside where it didn't show.

Once in a while, however, Donnie would get bored in the apartment and say, "Come on, let's play checkers, Jeff."

They would talk and laugh over a game and really have fun together. Jeff wished they could always be friends this way but it didn't seem possible.

One evening when the family was all sitting at the supper table, Donnie said, "I'd like to learn to play the saxophone. I saw an ad for one in a magazine today. It looks easy and I could practice it because I have to stay in the house all the time anyway."

"A saxophone!" Dad exclaimed. "You had a violin once and that was just money thrown away. I'm not going to buy another instrument for you."

Donnie didn't say any more about the saxophone but Jeff could see that he was both angry and disappointed.

On the way home from school the next day Jeff met Donnie and he looked happier. He was holding something bright and shiny in his mouth and making music come from it.

It wasn't a saxophone but a harmonica!

"Where'd you get it?" Jeff asked, walking faster to keep up with Donnie.

"Oh, from a friend!" Donnie stopped playing only long enough to answer. He was pretty good at it. The song almost sounded like *The Star-Spangled Banner.*

They marched into the store. Dad was behind the counter, straightening some shelves.

"Hello, boys," he greeted them. There was something serious about his manner. "I've been waiting to see you. You know how I always leave my wallet and my money on the bureau before I go to bed at night?"

The boys nodded their heads but didn't quite understand what Dad was leading up to.

"Well, I counted over my money this morning and there was a dollar missing," Dad went on. "I wondered if you boys saw it—" Dad's eyes fell on Donnie's bright harmonica suddenly. "Where did you get that?" he asked.

"I—I bought it from a fellow in my class," Donnie answered but

his voice was faltering.

Dad stared at the harmonica and then he looked at Donnie. "You were begging me for a saxophone last night and I said I wouldn't buy one for you. Donnie, did you take money from my bureau and buy this instead?"

The door of the store opened before Donnie could answer. A customer came in and Dad said hurriedly to Donnie, "If what I asked you is true you're going to get the spanking of your life! Go upstairs and wait for me until I can come up!"

His voice was such a command that both boys jumped to obey him.

"I didn't take any dollar—I didn't!" Donnie cried to Jeff as they climbed the stairs together.

Jeff didn't know what to answer. Dad had sounded angry, as if he was sure to spank Donnie. The boys reached the apartment and went inside. Mom wasn't home. Jeff remembered her saying that she was going shopping with Mrs. Jarecki this afternoon. Mom and Mrs. Jarecki were becoming more and more friendly all the time.

"I bought a harmonica from a guy in my class," Donnie said. "I gave him twenty-five cents for it and I owe him twenty-five more! I was going to ask Dad for it tonight."

"He'll never give it to you now!" Jeff answered knowingly.

"He thinks I took the dollar! He's going to whip me!" Donnie was on the verge of tears. "But I didn't take it—I didn't!" He went to the bed by the window and flung himself on it.

Jeff couldn't help feeling sorry for Donnie. Every time they heard a noise in the hall they thought it was Dad coming up. Jeff didn't know what to do. Who could have taken the money? he wondered. Could a burglar have come into the house last night? But they would have heard him. Dad would have chased him out!

Jeff wandered into the bedroom where Dad and Mom slept. There was the bureau where Dad always put his wallet and change at night. Jeff looked all over the top of it. He saw combs and brushes, a picture of Grandma in a frame, but no money.

He looked around the rest of the room. He got down on his hands and knees, searching under the bed, in all the corners, thinking he might find the missing dollar. He looked under the bureau. What was that way in the back? he wondered. It looked green—

"Donnie, I think I see some money on the floor way in back of the bureau!" he exclaimed. "Come help me!"

Donnie came running in. He didn't say anything but helped Jeff push the bureau away from the wall. They saw a crumpled green paper lying at their feet.

Jeff bent to pick it up. He smoothed the crumpled paper. He saw George Washington's face on a one-dollar bill.

"Dad must have dropped it!" he said. "It must have gotten kicked under the bureau. Show it to him, Donnie—"

"No, I don't want to talk to him!" Donnie began. "You show him—"

The door of the apartment opened just then. Jeff hurried out as Dad came in. "Your mother just came back, she's taking care of the store," Dad began. "Where's Donnie?"

"Look, Dad, I found the dollar!" Jeff held it out, his voice rising with excitement. "It must have fallen behind the bureau—"

Dad stared at the dollar. He came closer to Jeff and took the money from his hand. "Where did you get this?" he asked.

"I found it under the bureau. Come and see, I'll show you where."

Dad stood there, thoughtful for a moment. Then he looked up at Donnie who was standing in the bedroom doorway.

"Donnie, I shouldn't have said that you'd taken the money!" Dad began apologetically. "But I was upset by your wanting a saxophone and then when you came in with that harmonica, I thought you had bought it with that dollar."

Donnie didn't answer. He stood there, holding his chin high, but his lips were still trembling.

"Parents can be wrong, Donnie," Dad went on. "They worry about a lot of things, sometimes get angry, and take it out on their children. Donnie, I'm sorry. I'm not going to buy you a saxophone, but I'd like to make it up to you in some other way—"

"He bought the harmonica for a quarter and needs another quarter to finish paying for it," Jeff couldn't help saying.

"That's reasonable enough." Dad smiled softly. "I'll give you that other quarter. I hope you won't stay angry at me, the way you are now, that we'll be friends again," Dad said. He put his hand on Donnie's shoulder and then went downstairs.

Donnie didn't say anything for a while but then his voice came back. "It was swell of you—to find the dollar, Jeff. I—I might have gotten that spanking if you hadn't."

"That's—that's all right," Jeff gulped. Donnie had never talked to him this way. There was a closeness, an intimacy between them at this moment that they had never shared before.

"I—I'll try not to call you names anymore. Like 'Mary-Bessie—' and all that," Donnie went on. His face brightened considerably. He picked up the harmonica and started to play a tune.

They spent the rest of the afternoon together. Jeff knew that Donnie and he wouldn't be this close and friendly all the time. But if Donnie kept his promise and didn't call him names anymore that would be wonderful enough!

The Blue Willow Plate

BY DORIS GATES

Illustrated by Paul Lantz

"How long can we stay?" Janey Larkin always wondered
that for she and her father and Mom, her stepmother,
were constantly moving on as they followed the harvesting
of the crops. They had no real home. But Janey had a
secret dream—someday they would find a place where
she could ask her question and the answer would be
"As long as you want to." To Janey, her one treasure—
the blue willow plate that had belonged to her own mother
—was the symbol of that secret dream. Then the Larkins
came to the Anderson ranch, and Janey found a
friend in the neighbor's daughter, Lupe Romero.

Soon afterward trouble came. Mom was ill. There
was no money to pay the rent on their shack so Janey
bravely gave her treasured willow plate to Bounce, the
Anderson overseer, so they could stay a little longer.
But when the Larkins had to move on anyway, Janey
could not leave without one more look at her willow
plate. What happened next made Janey know that
sometimes dreams do come true.

THE NEXT two days were quite uneventful. Mom continued to
improve, Dad tried to find work, and Janey managed to take care of
Mom and to keep house with the neighborly help of Mrs. Romero. It
was good to be busy, so busy that at times she could almost forget
about the willow plate. Almost, but never entirely. There was some
small comfort in knowing that at last it had found a decent home.
For of course Janey believed that Bounce had turned it over to Mr.
Anderson, in whose name he had taken it.

104

On the third day, Miss Peterson came to call. The teacher at Lupe's school had turned out to be *the* Miss Peterson. Janey, answering the knock on the door and expecting to find one of the Romeros on the top step, was completely unprepared for the splendid surprise. For a moment she stood foolishly, unable to say a word.

"Howdy, Janey, won't you let me in?" Miss Peterson greeted her.

Janey flung the door wide and although a large slice of fog came in with the visitor, it seemed as if by some magic it had turned to pure sunshine. Miss Peterson could make everything different. Her arms were full of paper bags that bulged in an interesting way, and her face wore a broad smile.

"I would have come yesterday if I hadn't had to make a trip into Fresno. But I brought a few peace offerings with me."

Miss Peterson was putting the bundles on the table as she spoke and Janey, still rather dazed and trying to be helpful, proved so awkward that one of the bags upset, spilling sunshine in the form of oranges all over the room. In the scramble to pick them up, Miss Peterson managed to get acquainted with Mrs. Larkin and to put Janey at her ease.

It was rather late in the afternoon. Miss Peterson had had to wait until school was out before making her visit, so she hadn't been in the shack very long before Mr. Larkin came home. The minute he walked into the room, Janey knew something was troubling him, and something more than ordinarily disturbing. It would have to be pretty bad to make Dad look as sadly discouraged as he did now. It didn't take her long to decide what that something was. The work was gone. They would have to move. And there wasn't anything she could do about it, not anything at all. Not even the fact that Mom wouldn't be strong enough to travel for a long time could make any difference. They would have to go anyway.

Dad tried to throw off his gloom as he greeted Miss Peterson and thanked her for her gifts. But his smile was not very convincing, and his attempts at conversation even less so. After a few moments, Miss Peterson rose and went over to the bed.

"As soon as you are able to spare her, I want Janey to come to school," she told Mrs. Larkin.

Janey, hearing the words that once would have meant so much to her, was surprised to find that now they had no meaning whatsoever except to mock this moment. She found herself wishing they might have been left unsaid. But, of course, Miss Peterson had spoken them sincerely. She couldn't possibly know what Janey knew. And suddenly, looking at Miss Peterson, so friendly and so kind, and still thinking of what she had said, Janey didn't regret those words, after all. They made her feel somehow on the edge of belonging and a little closer to Lupe and the willow plate.

Dad moved over to the window and spoke without turning round.

"There's no use her starting school now," he said. "As soon as my wife is able to travel, and maybe before that, we'll be leaving. There's no more work around here and we've got to be heading toward the Imperial if we don't want to lose out all around."

"I understand," was all Miss Peterson said as she reached for her coat. At the door, she paused to give Janey a hug. "I'll see you again soon," she promised.

And she did. It was on Christmas Day, and again her arms were full of bundles. Janey hadn't thought much about its being Christmas.

Mom was getting a little stronger every day, and of course Janey was glad of that, but she knew all the time that when Mom was able to leave her bed, they would load up the car and be on their way. Dr. Pierce had said they must wait a month, but Dad couldn't wait that long. They would have to chance it, taking the best care of Mom they could. The money in the buckskin bag was running low, and they must move on while there was still enough left to buy gasoline and the things they would need before Dad found work again. So Janey knew that this visit of Miss Peterson's would be the last time they would see each other, most likely. Miss Peterson knew it too. And though she and Janey tried to be gay and to make believe they would meet again next summer, they each knew it was really good-by. So it wasn't a very merry Christmas in spite of the bundles.

At last one day Dad announced quietly: "We'll be on our way to-morrow."

They were finally spoken, the words Janey for three long months had been dreading to hear. Tomorrow they were going away from the Romeros, away from Miss Peterson and the "regular" school, and away from the willow plate. Never before had Janey left so much behind her. Never again would she want so much to stay.

On that last afternoon, with everything packed and ready to put into the car, Janey came to a sudden decision. She couldn't leave without one more look at the willow plate. It just wasn't possible to go away, perhaps forever, without telling the willow plate good-by.

Neither Mom nor Dad paid any attention to her when she put on her blue coat and slipped outdoors. Probably they thought she was going over for a last visit with Lupe. Janey was thankful that they asked no questions.

It was cold, bitterly cold. The fog lay close about her, collecting in tiny beads on the rough surface of her coat. She couldn't see more than fifty yards ahead of her, but she followed along by the barbed-wire fence in the direction of the Anderson place. When she came to the slough she skirted it and headed north, hoping to come upon the little road she had seen leading away from the old wooden bridge that day of her first visit. After much walking she came upon it. Turning to the right, she kept to the road until she came at last to the bridge. Here she paused for a moment to look back along the river. How changed everything was! The willows were no longer leafy and frond-like. Their bare branches were mere lines etched in criss-cross patterns against the fog. The water was as silent as before, but gray and cold and uninviting. Janey shivered and hurried on.

The ranch house was unchanged, however. It looked as weather-beaten and friendly as ever. Danger, the dog, was nowhere in sight.

Straight up to the front steps Janey went, and knocked on the door. In just a moment it was opened and an astonished woman asked Janey what she wanted.

"I want to talk to Mr. Anderson, please," Janey answered.

"Won't you come in?" The woman, who Janey guessed must be Mrs. Anderson, stepped aside, and her small visitor walked resolutely in.

Janey found herself in a large room with chairs scattered about it in welcoming positions, their outstretched arms inviting her to be comfortable. One of them had been turned completely around to face the hearth, where a fire danced brightly. She could see the top of a man's head above the chair back, and she hoped this would turn out to be Mr. Anderson. It did. As soon as the woman said: "Someone to see you, Nils," the head moved, a tall body rose out of the chair, and Mr. Anderson turned to face his caller.

"Hello," he said at sight of Janey. "Won't you sit down and tell me what I can do for you?"

Janey backed over to a chair and settled herself gingerly on the very edge of it. Her resoluteness seemed to have deserted her. Now that she was actually inside the Anderson house, the strangeness of her mission suddenly dawned upon her. What would Mr. Anderson think of her wanting to see the willow plate again? It was no longer any concern of hers. It belonged to him now. He might even be angry at this intrusion. She was a little uneasy as she began to speak.

"I guess you don't remember me," she faltered. "I'm Janey Larkin and once I came here to this place and Bounce and I quarreled and you came along and said I could have a dozen eggs."

All at once the politely inquiring look vanished from Mr. Anderson's face and a smile of remembering lit it up. "Of course. This is the

little girl I was telling you about," he said, turning to his wife. "This
is Mrs. Anderson, Janey."

"Pleased to meet you," said Janey, and ducked her head.

"You and Bounce haven't had more difficulty, have you, Janey?"
Mr. Anderson chuckled good-humoredly.

Janey shook her head. "I've come to tell the willow plate good-by.
We're going away tomorrow and I couldn't bear to go without seeing
it once more."

Mr. Anderson looked puzzled. "The willow plate?" he asked vaguely. "What willow plate?" He glanced questioningly at his wife, but
Janey saw that she was as puzzled as he, and cold fear gripped her
heart. Surely they weren't going to let on they didn't know about
the plate!

"Yes," pursued Janey, resolute once more, "don't you remember I
told you about it that day I was here? And Bounce took it a while
ago for the rent."

"Bounce!" Mr. Anderson fairly barked the name and Janey jumped so she nearly fell off the edge of her chair. "What's Bounce got to do with all this?"

"Why," exclaimed Janey, wonderingly, "Bounce is the one who collects your rent for you! We didn't have the money last time, so we gave him the willow plate instead."

Mr. and Mrs. Anderson's eyes met over Janey's head. The air seemed to be full of question marks. Mr. Anderson's face was suddenly so full of anger that Janey rose. Evidently they didn't want her to see the willow plate, after all. But the man put out a hand. "Sit down," he said, kindly. "Suppose you tell me the whole story from the very beginning. I want all of it."

Deciding she had nothing to fear and glad that at last she could put her trust in this man just as she had wanted to do that day under the willows, Janey once more perched herself on the edge of her chair and began her story. She told it straightforwardly and simply without any emphasis on any particular part. Except when Dad won second prize in the contest and then a note of pride did creep into her voice.

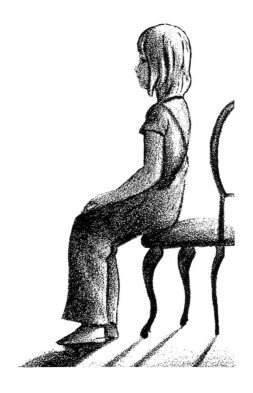

"We got this coat with some of the money," she said in an aside to Mrs. Anderson.

"And a very pretty one it is," was her reply.

They exchanged knowing smiles with each other, quite ignoring Mr. Anderson, since no man could be expected to appreciate a thing like that.

"Why didn't you come to me before?" Mr. Anderson asked when Janey had finished.

"There was no reason to come," said Janey. "I wouldn't be here now if I hadn't wanted to see the willow plate once more."

"Well, you see, Janey, I didn't know anything about the rent. Whatever money Bounce got from you, he kept. I have never seen the willow plate." Mr. Anderson paused for a moment, frowning at the floor. "But I intend to see it very soon," he added in a tone which Janey was certain boded no good for Bounce Reyburn.

But in the meantime where was the willow plate? All this talk about the Larkins and about Bounce and his dishonesty only mildly interested Janey. She had come to see the plate.

"I think the plate will have to wait a little while," Mr. Anderson replied to her question. "I want to talk to your father before I talk to Bounce." He rose and stood looking down at the small girl. "It wouldn't surprise me a bit, Janey, if you didn't pull out of here tomorrow."

"Honest?" cried Janey, jumping to her feet, her blue eyes dancing.

Mr. Anderson chuckled quietly. "You're a funny little coot," was all he said, but Janey liked the way he said it.

Janey hadn't noticed when Mrs. Anderson left the room, but now she appeared wearing a hat and coat.

"I'm going with you to the Larkins', Nils," she said.

"Good," replied her husband, heartily. "I'll get the car."

Janey never forgot that ride back to the shack. She sat between Mr. and Mrs. Anderson. They hardly spoke, but the air was full of suspense, a nice kind of suspense holding the promise that everything was going to be all right. Janey could feel the sympathy of these two grown-ups. She even stopped worrying about the willow plate. She knew the Andersons would see that she got it again. She hoped Dad

wouldn't be cross with her for going to the Anderson ranch alone. She supposed she should have asked leave to go, but suppose he had refused to allow her? Suppose they had just gone away tomorrow without ever saying a word to Mr. Anderson? They would have lost the willow plate forever. Janey shuddered at the thought, and Mrs. Anderson tucked the lap robe closer around her, thinking she was cold.

"Anyway," thought Janey, "it will be worth a scolding, a good hard one, to have the willow plate back."

But Janey didn't get a scolding, not that evening anyway. For with Nils Anderson's visit to the shack, the lives and fortunes of the Larkins were changed. Never again would they be wanderers upon the earth, never again would Janey long in vain to go to a "regular" school. Mr. Anderson was shown the receipts which Bounce had signed and which were positive proof of his dishonesty. Long and earnestly the two men talked while the women and Janey listened. Darkness settled down over the land, and Mr. Larkin rose and lit the gasoline lantern and the talking continued. Much of it was about the ranch in the Dust Bowl and about their lives before the drought forced the Larkins to leave Texas.

Mr. Anderson listened intently, interrupting only when Janey's father had reached the place in his story where the Larkins had taken refuge in the shack.

"I guess we shouldn't have done that, but you forget about such fine points when you live as we do," Mr. Larkin said.

The other man gestured impatiently. "Of course you should have done it. You're not the first family to occupy this shack. It has no value except to people like you, and anyone has been welcome to use it who wanted to. As far as that goes, I knew somebody was in it this fall, because I had seen you around here when I came over this way, and I had no objections to your staying. Of course I'd no idea of what Bounce was up to. He's probably been grafting on everyone who moved in here."

Mr. Anderson's face was set in hard, bitter lines. Janey couldn't help wishing Bounce would walk in now. It would be entirely different from that other night when he had been so sure of himself, and Dad had seemed at his mercy.

"Well, that's about all the story," Dad said after an interval of silence, rubbing his palms together in a slow, uncertain way.

Following his words, the silence continued, broken only by the rasping sound of his callused palms.

Everyone else sat motionless. Once the fire snapped loudly and out in the field a cow bawled. Janey, sitting cross-legged in the middle of the floor, looked anxiously from one face to another. Her father and mother were sitting on the edge of the bed, their eyes staring unseeingly before them. Plainly, Dad was talked out. It would be up to Mr. Anderson now.

Janey saw him exchange a look with his wife. Mrs. Anderson's head nodded slowly. With sudden decision, Mr. Anderson got to his feet.

"I'm letting Bounce go tomorrow, Larkin. I'll need a man in his place. The job is yours if you want it. Seventy-five dollars a month, a house, and all the eggs and milk you can use."

Mr. Larkin lifted his head and looked at Mr. Anderson in a dazed way. The offer was repeated. Slowly, awkwardly, Mr. Larkin got to his feet and put out his hand. He didn't say a word, and Janey was terrified for fear Mr. Anderson would think Dad didn't want the job. She wanted to scream to her father to say something, quick, before it should be too late. But Janey had learned during her strange life that there are times when only men are important, when even grown-up women don't matter at all. And certainly not little girls. This was distinctly one of those times. So she held her tongue and waited in an agony of suspense for whatever might happen.

It was with infinite relief that she saw Mr. Anderson grasp her father's hand, heard him say in friendly tones: "Take it easy there, Larkin. You deserve a break and I'm glad I can give it to you. I'll expect you to move in tomorrow."

There were almost no other words spoken, for the simple reason that there was nothing more anyone could say. Besides, this thing which had just happened to them struck the Larkins' hearts too deeply for chatter. They were unequal, even, to the obvious necessity of expressing gratitude. But, happily, it wasn't expected of them. The Andersons hastily said good-night and went away.

After they had gone, Mom spoke at last, looking squarely at Dad.

"What he said was the truth. You do deserve a break. I'm glad it's come."

Dad reached out and drew Janey down on his knee, holding her close.

"I guess we have Janey to thank for it," he said.

Mom studied the two of them for a moment, then shook her head. "We should give thanks to that Power which is greater than Janey, greater than all of us."

Dad didn't reply, and Janey wondered as she felt his cheek against her head whether Mom meant God or the willow plate. Just to be safe, she offered up a silent prayer to both.

Hold Fast Your Dreams

BY LOUISE DRISCOLL

Illustrated by Katherine Grace

Hold fast your dreams!
Within your heart
Keep one still, secret spot
Where dreams may go,
And sheltered so,
May thrive and grow—
Where doubt and fear are not.
Oh, keep a place apart
Within your heart
For little dreams to go.

117

Andre

BY GWENDOLYN BROOKS

Illustrated by Judith Quinn

I had a dream last night. I dreamed
I had to pick a Mother out.
I had to choose a Father too.
At first I wondered what to do,
There were so many there, it seemed,
Short and tall and thin and stout.

But just before I sprang awake,
I knew what parents I would take.

And *this* surprised and made me glad!
They were the ones I always had!

Henry and Ribs

BY BEVERLY CLEARY

Illustrated by Katherine Grace

Henry Huggins was a boy who felt that nothing exciting
ever happened to him. Then one day he went downtown
and met a hungry dog that he named Ribs. After that,
everything seemed to happen to Henry! Here is
one of his funny adventures.

H ENRY HUGGINS was in the fourth grade. His hair looked like
a scrubbing brush and most of his grown-up front teeth were in. He
lived with his mother and father in a square white house on Klickitat Street. Except for having his tonsils out when he was six and
breaking his arm falling out of a cherry tree when he was seven,
nothing much happened to Henry.

I wish something exciting would happen, Henry often thought.

But nothing very interesting ever happened to Henry, at least not
until one Wednesday afternoon in March. Every Wednesday after
school Henry rode downtown on the bus to go swimming at the
Y.M.C.A. After he swam for an hour, he got on the bus again and
rode home just in time for dinner. It was fun but not really exciting. 119

When Henry left the Y.M.C.A. on this particular Wednesday, he stopped to watch a man tear down a circus poster. Then, with three nickels and one dime in his pocket, he went to the corner drugstore to buy a chocolate ice cream cone. He thought he would eat the ice cream cone, get on the bus, drop his dime in the slot, and ride home.

That is not what happened.

He bought the ice cream cone and paid for it with one of his nickels. On his way out of the drugstore he stopped to look at funny books. It was a free look, because he had only two nickels left.

He stood there licking his chocolate ice cream cone and reading one of the funny books when he heard a thump, thump, thump. Henry turned, and there behind him was a dog. The dog was scratching himself. He wasn't any special kind of dog. He was too small to be a big dog but, on the other hand, he was much too big to be a little dog. He wasn't a white dog, because parts of him were brown and other parts were black and in between there were yellowish patches. His ears stood up and his tail was long and thin.

The dog was hungry. When Henry licked, he licked. When Henry swallowed, he swallowed.

"Hello, you old dog," Henry said. "You can't have my ice cream cone."

Swish, swish, swish went the tail. "Just one bite," the dog's brown eyes seemed to say.

"Go away," ordered Henry. He wasn't very firm about it. He patted the dog's head.

The tail wagged harder. Henry took one last lick. "Oh, all right," he said. "If you're that hungry, you might as well have it."

The ice cream cone disappeared in one gulp.

"Now go away," Henry told the dog. "I have to catch a bus for home."

He started for the door. The dog started, too.

"Go away, you skinny old dog." Henry didn't say it very loudly. "Go on home."

The dog sat down at Henry's feet. Henry looked at the dog and the dog looked at Henry.

"I don't think you've got a home. You're awful thin. Your ribs show right through your skin."

Thump, thump, thump replied the tail.

"And you haven't got a collar," said Henry.

He began to think. If only he could keep the dog! He had always wanted a dog of his very own and now he had found a dog that wanted him. He couldn't go home and leave a hungry dog on the street corner. If only he knew what his mother and father would say! He fingered the two nickels in his pocket. That was it! He would use one of the nickels to phone his mother.

"Come on, Ribsy. Come on, Ribs, old boy. I'm going to call you Ribsy because you're so thin."

The dog trotted after the boy to the telephone booth in the corner of the drugstore. Henry shoved him into the booth and shut the door. He had never used a pay telephone before. He had to put the telephone book on the floor and stand on tiptoe on it to reach the mouthpiece. He gave the operator his number and dropped his nickel into the coin box.

"Hello—Mom?"

"Why, Henry!" His mother sounded surprised. "Where are you?" 121

"At the drugstore near the Y."

Ribs began to scratch. Thump, thump, thump. Inside the telephone booth the thumps sounded loud and hollow.

"For goodness' sake, Henry, what's that noise?" his mother demanded. Ribs began to whimper and then howl. "Henry," Mrs. Huggins shouted, "are you all right?"

"Yes, I'm all right," Henry shouted back. He never could understand why his mother always thought something had happened to him when nothing ever did. "That's just Ribsy."

"Ribsy?" His mother was exasperated. "Henry, will you please tell me what is going on?"

"I'm trying to," said Henry. Ribsy howled louder. People were gathering around the phone booth to see what was going on. "Mother, I've found a dog. I sure wish I could keep him. He's a good dog and I'd feed him and wash him and everything. Please, Mom."

"I don't know, dear," his mother said. "You'll have to ask your father."

"Mom!" Henry wailed. "That's what you always say!" Henry was tired of standing on tiptoe and the phone booth was getting warm. "Mom, please say yes and I'll never ask for another thing as long as I live!"

"Well, all right, Henry. I guess there isn't any reason why you shouldn't have a dog. But you'll have to bring him home on the bus. Your father has the car today and I can't come after you. Can you manage?"

"Sure! Easy."

"And Henry, please don't be late. It looks as if it might rain."

"All right, Mom." Thump, thump, thump.

"Henry, what's that thumping noise?"

"It's my dog, Ribsy. He's scratching a flea."

"Oh, Henry," Mrs. Huggins moaned. "Couldn't you have found a dog without fleas?"

Henry thought that was a good time to hang up. "Come on, Ribs," he said. "We're going home on the bus."

When the big green bus stopped in front of the drugstore, Henry picked up his dog. Ribsy was heavier than he expected. He had a hard time getting him into the bus and was wondering how he would get a dime out of his pocket when the driver said, "Say, sonny, you can't take that dog on the bus."

"Why not?" asked Henry.

"It's a company rule, sonny. No dogs on buses."

"Golly, Mister, how'm I going to get him home? I just have to get him home."

"Sorry, sonny. I didn't make the rule. No animal can ride on a bus unless it's inside a box."

"Well, thanks anyway," said Henry doubtfully, and lifted Ribsy off the bus.

"Well, I guess we'll have to get a box. I'll get you onto the next bus somehow," promised Henry.

He went back into the drugstore followed closely by Ribsy. "Have you got a big box I could have, please?" he asked the man at the toothpaste counter. "I need one big enough for my dog."

The clerk leaned over the counter to look at Ribsy. "A cardboard box?" he asked.

"Yes, please," said Henry, wishing the man would hurry. He didn't want to be late getting home.

The clerk pulled a box out from under the counter. "This hair tonic carton is the only one I have. I guess it's big enough, but why anyone would want to put a dog in a cardboard box I can't understand."

The box was about two feet square and six inches deep. On one end was printed, "Don't Let Them Call You Baldy," and on the other, "Try Our Large Economy Size."

Henry thanked the clerk, carried the box out to the bus stop, and put it on the sidewalk. Ribsy padded after him. "Get in, fellow," Henry commanded. Ribsy understood. He stepped into the box and sat down just as the bus came around the corner. Henry had to kneel to pick up the box. It was not a very strong box and he had to put his arms under it. He staggered as he lifted it, feeling like the strong man who lifted weights at the circus. Ribsy lovingly licked his face with his wet pink tongue.

"Hey, cut that out!" Henry ordered. "You better be good if you're going to ride on the bus with me."

The bus stopped at the curb. When it was Henry's turn to get on, he had trouble finding the step because he couldn't see his feet. He had to try several times before he hit it. Then he discovered he had forgotten to take his dime out of his pocket. He was afraid to put the box down for fear Ribsy might escape.

He turned sideways to the driver and asked politely, "Will you please take the dime out of my pocket for me? My hands are full."

The driver pushed his cap back on his head and exclaimed, "Full! I should say they *are* full! And just where do you think you're going with that animal?"

"Home," said Henry in a small voice.

The passengers were staring and most of them were smiling. The box was getting heavier every minute.

"Not on this bus, you're not!" said the driver.

"But the man on the last bus said I could take the dog on the bus in a box," protested Henry, who was afraid he couldn't hold the dog much longer. "He said it was a company rule."

"He meant a big box tied shut. A box with holes punched in it for the dog to breathe through."

Henry was horrified to hear Ribsy growl. "Shut up," he ordered.

Ribsy began to scratch his left ear with his left hind foot. The box began to tear. Ribsy jumped out of the box and off the bus and Henry jumped after him. The bus pulled away with a puff of exhaust.

"Now see what you've done! You've spoiled everything." The dog hung his head and tucked his tail between his legs. "If I can't get you home, how can I keep you?"

Henry sat down on the curb to think. It was so late and the clouds were so dark that he didn't want to waste time looking for a big box. His mother was probably beginning to worry about him.

People were stopping on the corner to wait for the next bus. Among them Henry noticed an elderly lady carrying a large paper shopping bag full of apples. The shopping bag gave him an idea. Jumping up, he snapped his fingers at Ribs and ran back into the drugstore.

"You back again?" asked the toothpaste clerk. "What do you want   125 this time? String and paper to wrap your dog in?"

"No, sir," said Henry. "I want one of those big nickel shopping bags." He laid his last nickel on the counter.

"Well, I'll be darned," said the clerk, and handed the bag across the counter.

Henry opened the bag and set it up on the floor. He picked up Ribsy and shoved him hind feet first into the bag. Then he pushed his front feet in. A lot of Ribsy was left over.

The clerk was leaning over the counter watching. "I guess I'll have to have some string and paper, too," Henry said, "if I can have some free."

"Well! Now I've seen everything." The clerk shook his head as he handed a piece of string and a big sheet of paper across the counter.

Ribsy whimpered, but he held still while Henry wrapped the paper loosely around his head and shoulders and tied it with the string. The dog made a lumpy package, but by taking one handle of the bag in each hand Henry was able to carry it to the bus stop. He didn't think the bus driver would notice him. It was getting dark and a crowd of people, most of them with packages, was waiting on the corner. A few spatters of rain hit the pavement.

This time Henry remembered his dime. Both hands were full, so he held the dime in his teeth and stood behind the woman with the bag of apples. Ribsy wiggled and whined, even though Henry tried to pet him through the paper. When the bus stopped, he climbed on behind the lady, quickly set the bag down, dropped his dime in the slot, picked up the bag, and squirmed through the crowd to a seat beside a fat man near the back of the bus.

"Whew!" Henry sighed with relief. The driver was the same one he had met on the first bus! But Ribs was on the bus at last. Now if he could only keep him quiet for fifteen minutes they would be home and Ribsy would be his for keeps.

The next time the bus stopped Henry saw Scooter McCarthy, a fifth grader at school, get on and make his way through the crowd to the back of the bus.

Just my luck, thought Henry. I'll bet he wants to know what's in my bag.

"Hi," said Scooter.

"Hi," said Henry.

"Whatcha got in that bag?" asked Scooter.

"None of your beeswax," answered Henry.

Scooter looked at Henry. Henry looked at Scooter. Crackle, crackle, crackle went the bag. Henry tried to hold it more tightly between his knees.

"There's something alive in that bag!" Scooter said accusingly.

"Shut up, Scooter!" whispered Henry.

"Aw, shut up yourself!" said Scooter. "You've got something alive in that bag!"

By this time the passengers at the back of the bus were staring at Henry and his package. Crackle, crackle, crackle. Henry tried to pat Ribsy again through the paper. The bag crackled even louder. Then it began to wiggle.

"Come on, tell us what's in the bag," coaxed the fat man.

"N-n-n-nothing," stammered Henry. "Just something I found."

"Maybe it's a rabbit," suggested one passenger. "I think it's kicking."

"No, it's too big for a rabbit," said another.

"I'll bet it's a baby," said Scooter. "I'll bet you kidnaped a baby!"

"I did not!"

Ribs began to whimper and then to howl. Crackle, crackle, crackle. Thump, thump, thump. Ribsy scratched his way out of the bag.

"Well, I'll be doggoned!" exclaimed the fat man and began to laugh. "I'll be doggoned!"

"It's just a skinny old dog," said Scooter.

"He is not! He's a good dog."

Henry tried to keep Ribsy between his knees. The bus lurched around a corner and started to go uphill. Henry was thrown against the fat man. The frightened dog wiggled away from him, squirmed between the passengers, and started for the front of the bus.

"Here, Ribsy, old boy! Come back here," called Henry and started after him.

"E-e-ek! A dog!" squealed the lady with the bag of apples. "Go   127 away, doggie, go away!"

Ribsy was scared. He tried to run and crashed into the lady's bag of apples. The bag tipped over and the apples began to roll toward the back of the bus, which was grinding up a steep hill. The apples rolled around the feet of the people who were standing. Passengers began to slip and slide. They dropped their packages and grabbed one another.

Crash! A high-school girl dropped an armload of books.

Rattle! Bang! Crash! A lady dropped a big paper bag. The bag broke open and pots and pans rolled out.

Thud! A man dropped a coil of garden hose. The hose unrolled and the passengers found it wound around their legs.

People were sitting on the floor. They were sitting on books and apples. They were even sitting on other people's laps. Some of them had their hats over their faces and their feet in the air.

Skree-e-etch! The driver threw on the brakes and turned around in his seat just as Henry made his way through the apples and books and pans and hose to catch Ribsy.

The driver pushed his cap back on his head. "O.K., sonny," he said to Henry. "Now you know why dogs aren't allowed on buses!"

"Yes, sir," said Henry in a small voice. "I'm sorry."

"You're sorry! A lot of good that does. Look at this bus! Look at those people!"

"I didn't mean to make any trouble," said Henry. "My mother said I could keep the dog if I could bring him home on the bus."

The fat man began to snicker. Then he chuckled. Then he laughed and then he roared. He laughed until tears streamed down his cheeks and all the other passengers were laughing too, even the man with the hose and the lady with the apples.

The driver didn't laugh. "Take that dog and get off the bus!" he   129 ordered. Ribsy whimpered and tucked his tail between his legs.

The fat man stopped laughing. "See here, driver," he said, "you can't put that boy and his dog off in the rain."

"Well, he can't stay on the bus," snapped the driver.

Henry didn't know what he was going to do. He guessed he'd have to walk the rest of the way home. He wasn't sure he knew the way in the dark.

Just then a siren screamed. It grew louder and louder until it stopped right alongside the bus.

A policeman appeared in the entrance. "Is there a boy called Henry Huggins on this bus?" he asked.

"Oh boy, you're going to be arrested for having a dog on the bus!" gloated Scooter. "I'll bet you have to go to jail!"

"I'm him," said Henry in a very small voice.

"I am he," corrected the lady with the apples, who had been a schoolteacher and couldn't help correcting boys.

"You'd better come along with us," said the policeman.

"Boy, you're sure going to get it!" said Scooter.

"Surely going to get it," corrected the apple lady.

Henry and Ribsy followed the policeman off the bus and into the squad car, where Henry and the dog sat in the back seat.

"Are you going to arrest me?" Henry asked timidly.

"Well, I don't know. Do you think you ought to be arrested?"

"No, sir," said Henry politely. He thought the policeman was joking, but he wasn't sure. It was hard to tell about grownups sometimes. "I didn't mean to do anything. I just had to get Ribsy home. My mother said I could keep him if I could bring him home on the bus."

"What do you think?" the officer asked his partner, who was driving the squad car.

"We-e-ell, I think we might let him off this time," answered the driver. "His mother must be pretty worried about him if she called the police, and I don't think she'd want him to go to jail."

"Yes, he's late for his dinner already. Let's see how fast we can get him home."

The driver pushed a button and the siren began to shriek. Ribsy raised his head and howled. The tires sucked at the wet pavement and the windshield wipers splip-splopped. Henry began to enjoy himself. Wouldn't this be something to tell the kids at school! Automobiles pulled over to the curb as the police car went faster and faster. Even the bus Henry had been on had to pull over and stop. Henry waved to the passengers. They waved back. Up the hill the police car sped and around the corner until they came to Klickitat Street and then to Henry's block and then pulled up in front of his house.

Henry's mother and father were standing on the porch waiting for him. The neighbors were looking out of their windows.

"Well!" said his father after the policeman had gone. "It's about time you came home. So this is Ribsy! I've heard about you, fellow, and there's a big bone and a can of Feeley's Flea Flakes waiting for you."

"Henry, what *will* you do next?" sighed his mother.

"Golly, Mom, I didn't do anything. I just brought my dog home on the bus like you said."

Ribsy sat down and began to scratch.

The Horseman

BY WALTER DE LA MARE

Illustrated by Katherine Grace

I heard a horseman
  Ride over the hill;
The moon shone clear,
  The night was still;
His helm was silver,
  And pale was he;
And the horse he rode
  Was of ivory.

Robin Saves the Day

BY MARGUERITE DE ANGELI

Illustrated by Marguerite de Angeli

Robin lived in England during the fourteenth century.
"Forget not to be brave," his soldier father, Sir John
de Bureford, told him, riding off to the wars. But
while his father was away, a strange disease crippled
Robin. How could a lame boy be a brave knight?
Robin did not find the answer until he became a page
to Sir Peter and great Lindsay Castle was besieged.
It was Adam the Yeoman who spoke the words that
gave Robin the idea of how to save the castle—
and Robin soon learned that a brave heart counts
more than crippled legs.

"SOMEONE must go for help," Adam said, "or we shall be forced to surrender the castle. It might be that Sir Hugh Fitzhugh would come to our aid, for he, too, is in danger from the Welsh if they break our defense. But whom shall we spare? All are needed at their posts."

"Let me go," said Robin. "I can go out the small door at the north whilst it is early morning. No one will suspect me. They think me a poor shepherd. I shall borrow a smock from William the Farrier's son, and if I am seen, I shall appear stupid. We shall keep it secret, for if Sir Peter were to find out my plan he would forbid me to go, not knowing how strong I am."

"But thou'rt only a lad!" Adam objected, "and art cumbered with crutches as well. And how wilt thou cross the river? The bridge is well guarded at both ends."

"I shall go well, never fear," Robin assured them confidently. "I have it all in my head how it shall be done. I shall find John-go-in-the-Wynd at his mother's cottage in Tripheath village. John shall set forth from there for Sir Hugh and his men. Now, let us plan. First, I want you, Denis, to bring me the smock, and some rags to wrap about my legs. Then, see you, find me a hood that is worn and faded. Besides, I shall need long leather thongs to tie the crutches to my back, for I shall swim the river."

"Fear you not the soldiery?" queried Denis anxiously. "Will you not fall down the steep bank? 'Tis a far distance to the bottom of the ravine, and——" He stopped suddenly, because one of the maids appeared.

"See to it," said Robin with a quick nod.

That evening there was no gathering about the fire. Everyone was restless. The hounds were still uneasy, walking about, cocking their ears at the least sound.

Lady Constance took one of her women to examine the stores. Robin was afraid she would discover how low the water was in the well. Instead, she seemed confident that there was sufficient.

"How fortunate we are that there is plenty of water," she said. "Sir Peter says that our well has never failed."

Denis looked at Robin, knowing that he shared the secret.

Denis, knowing Robin's plan, was in a fidget to be through with his duties and find William the Farrier's son and borrow his clothes. He would probably be with his father at the forge, repairing pikes and lances and heating oil for pouring onto the enemy in case they should pierce the outer castle wall.

Robin put on his warmest under tunic and carefully put away the little harp and all the parts and tools so that they would be safe. He looked at it regretfully, hating to leave it.

Then, when all was ready except changing his clothes, he sought out Brother Luke, for he knew that the friar would give him help and encouragement.

Dressed in the patched and ragged smock, his legs wound about with bits of rag to hold the ill-fitting hosen, Robin tried to sleep away the early part of the night, but excitement kept him wakeful. Even

when he dozed, he was aware of what he was about to do. He counted over all the things he must remember. He must go softly with the crutches. He must remember the leather thongs. As Brother Luke had told him, he mustn't forget oil for the rusty lock of the door in the wall. He must keep D'Ath quiet.

Just before dawn Brother Luke touched him.

"Come, my son," he whispered. "We shall say the office before it is time to set forth on thy mission."

When the prayers were finished, Robin pulled on the faded hood, tucked the leather thong inside it, and followed the friar. D'Ath rose from sleep to follow after, but Robin touched his head and whispered a command for him to stop.

"D'Ath, stay you here," he said, wishing very much that the dog could go with him.

They went down a half flight of steps and across the hall of the keep to the winding stair, making their way quietly among the sleeping servants. They went very slowly, for Robin's crutches tapped an alarm when he made haste, and the least misstep would have sent him clattering down.

There was still fog when they came into the open, but it had begun to drift and there was a gray dawn just beginning to break.

"Who goes there?" demanded the sentry at the door, but seeing Robin and the friar, he allowed them to pass, thinking they were bent on some holy errand.

Robin shuddered.

"Art fearful, my son?" asked the friar.

"Not truly," answered Robin, "though 'tis weird in the fog."

"Aye, 'tis an eerie feeling to be out in the cheerless dawn, not knowing at what moment an enemy may appear out of the fog," agreed Brother Luke. And at that moment a face did appear, but it was only one of the guards, who thought the two were on their way to the chapel.

They reached the sally port in the north wall without meeting anyone else. Brother Luke dripped oil into the lock before trying to open the door.

Robin listened.

"Hark!" he whispered. "I hear the Welsh sentry outside. We can count the paces and can tell how far away he is. One, two, three, four——" They counted forty paces. "Now!"

Slowly the door opened and Robin slipped outside.

"Benedicite," whispered the friar in blessing, and closed the door.

Quickly Robin moved away from the door and the wall. In a moment he was at the edge of the deep ravine. He could hear the river far below but could not see it for the fog.

Now began the dangerous descent. Carefully Robin tested each clod of earth, each bit of stone, before trusting his weight to the crutches, praying the while that the fog would hold. Sometimes he slid on his haunches, sometimes seedling trees held him till he was able to find sure footing.

"If I should start a stone rolling," he thought, "the whole Welsh army will be upon my neck."

It seemed hours to Robin that he was sliding, groping, laboring down the treacherous cliff, but it was only a few moments, for the light of morning had scarcely changed when he reached the bottom and found himself at the edge of the river.

He stopped only long enough to fasten the crutches onto his back with the leathern thong and to wind his hood into a kind of hat that perched on top of his head. Then he plunged into the icy water, not allowing himself to consider whether he had the courage to do it.

When first the water closed over him Robin thought he could not bear it. The crutches were awkward. His chest felt tightly squeezed, and as if sharp knives pierced him. He seemed unable to breathe, and his head felt ready to burst. But he struck out fiercely, and after a few strokes began to breathe more easily. Warmth crept through his body and a feeling of power, as if nothing could be too difficult for him. He swam strongly across the swift current toward the path he had seen from the top of the tower.

What if the enemy should be camped on the other side? Suppose they wouldn't believe he was the poor shepherd he pretended to be? Suppose he found it impossible to get up the bank on the other side?

"Anyone could *not* do it," he said to himself stubbornly, and thrashed his arms more fiercely.

At last he felt the stones of shallower water under his feet, the bank appeared mistily green, and he was able to hold himself steady with one hand while he untied the crutches and set them under his armpits. The bank was not very steep after all, and in a moment he was at the top, ready to go on. His teeth chattered in the rising wind.

His feet felt as if they had been frozen. His hands were so numb with cold he could hardly hold the crutches to steady them as he walked. He paused long enough to let down the hood into its proper shape. The warm wool felt good, although it was wet along the edges. Then he looked about for signs of the path. It had shown so clearly from the top of the tower. He moved along the bank a few paces where generations of peasants had worn a "highway," and soon came to the path. The fog was lifting somewhat with the wind, and Robin, looking back once, caught sight of the castle he had left behind. He even caught a glimpse of the sentry along the narrow ridge just where he had so lately escaped by the door in the wall.

After passing through a patch of brush and willows Robin came out into a field. He still could not see very far ahead, but the path was straight before him, so he began to swing along as fast as he could, his crutches making great sweeping circles, his feet covering the ground in tremendous strides. There seemed to be no one about,

137

so he made haste without regard to noise, and gradually the numbness in his hands and feet began to ease. Across the field he went, swing-step, swing-step, swing-step.

The fog wavered and lifted, swirled about in sudden drafts, floated across the path in thin layers, showed a patch of blue sky for an instant and glimpses of trees ahead.

Suddenly a voice rang out.

"*Who goes there?*"

Robin stopped.

" 'Tis but I, Robin," he answered in a meek voice, and the chill that ran down his spine was not all from the dampness of his clothing.

"Robin who?" the voice went on.

"Robin—Crookshank, some call me," answered Robin.

The fog parted, showing the fierce and scowling head of a man.

The guard drew near where he could see the boy.

"Aah," he said. "Art tha' but a shepherd boy, then?" he asked, seeing Robin's poor clothes. "And hast fallen into the river? Come, then, lad, and warm tha'self by the fire. Be not frighted. We'll not hurt thee." He took Robin's arm and tried to draw him toward the camp, which now Robin could see just at the side of the field, for now the fog was fast disappearing. But Robin held back and shook his head, trying to think what he must say and how he must speak.

"Nay," he began, trying to appear stupid, "'tis na far to the cottage." He edged away, bobbing his thanks, and went on as fast as he dared up the other side of the field and through the hedgerow. He did not stop until he was well beyond earshot of the men in the camp, then stood only for a moment to draw long, steadying breaths.

He chuckled at the way he had fooled the Welshman.

From that point on the path led through a wood and downward toward the valley of a stream which joined the one surrounding the castle. There were no cottages near at hand, but across the stream and beyond a low-lying field and a rising slope Robin could see the wood that extended to the edge of the village where the church tower stood. The sky now was filled with fast-flying clouds and the fog was gone. The stream was shallow enough for Robin to go across on foot and the little wetting he got was nothing after swimming the river.

The wood behind him hid Robin from the camp in the field, for which he was thankful, because the rising ground slowed his going, and he felt as if he were a fair target for arrows. It seemed as if he would never come to the top of the field and the hedgerow separating it from the forest beyond. When he reached the shelter of the great trees, Robin sank down into a bed of bracken to rest. He was very tired.

When breathing was easier and the pain of effort but a dull ache, Robin rose to go on. How much farther had he to go? Would John be there when he arrived? Would he be able to get help in time?

Even through the forest the path was well marked, because it was one that had been used for centuries. The peasants went over it to and from the villages to gather wood or to pasture the sheep.

In about an hour the forest began to thin, and Robin could see the blue smoke coming from the cotters' chimney pots. Which cottage belonged to John's mother? Robin remembered that John had said it was on the heath and near the church. He could see such a cottage from where he stood, so he made his way toward it hopefully. It was so exciting to be within sight of help that Robin forgot that he was tired and hungry; he forgot that he was still cold from his dousing in the river and the fright he'd had.

He began to cut across the heath toward the cottage but had not gone far when John himself came out of the door.

Robin stopped.

"John!" he called at the top of his voice. *"John! Oh, John*-go-in-the-Wy-y-y-nd."

John heard him and looked his way, then came running.

"Master Robin!" he exclaimed. "What's amiss? How came thou here?"

Without waiting for an answer he grasped Robin's crutches and swept him up into his arms, because he could see that Robin had come as far as he was able. It had been Robin's plan to issue orders as his father might have done; to have been lordly and commanding. But it was such a relief to be cared for and to have the weight of his body taken from his aching armpits that he allowed John to carry him, and said not a word until he was laid upon the straw pallet.

An old woman stood by the fire stirring something in a pot. She looked at Robin but didn't speak. A cat mewed and coaxed her, rubbing against her skirts.

"The castle is in danger!" said Robin at once. "The Welsh have taken the town and are at the gates of the outer bailey. The food is giving out. The water low in the well. You must get help. You must get it soon."

"But how came thou here?" said John, amazed. "How didst escape the sentry?" John was already putting on his hood and fastening his leather jerkin.

He went on without waiting.

"Knowest what force the Welsh have?"

"No," said Robin, "the fog has kept us from seeing. But whenever we tried to make a sally into the town, we were forced back."

"I shall be gone straight away. Stay thou here for safety and rest."

John-go-in-the-Wynd was well named, for go he did, closing the door behind him almost before he had finished speaking.

Robin sighed. It was good to be able to rest.

"Come, now," said the woman, as she took off Robin's clothes to dry them. "Thou'lt be famished with hunger. I'll bake thee a bannock." As tired as he was, Robin grinned. She went to the cupboard and took out a flat cake which she put on a hot stone to bake.

Robin slept after the woman fed him and didn't wake until the sun

was low in the west. The sound of the door opening was what really woke him. It was John.

Robin was up on his elbow in a second.

"Did you not go then?" he asked in bewilderment. Then he realized he had slept and that it was late in the day. "Did you find help then?"

"Yes, already they are well on their way from my lord Hugh Fitz-hugh's castle," said John. "A large force of foot soldiers and a company of lancers go by the drovers' road, one company by the way through wood and field and another going around to attack from the other side of the town by way of Letham Bridge. It hath been agreed that we shall give the signal from the bell tower of the church. There are no better bowmen in England. The siege will be lifted. Thou'lt see!"

"I want to see it," declared Robin. "I want to see it all!"

"See it thou shalt," promised John. "Now, Mither, serve forth yon porridge, for I have not broken my fast this day."

The mother bustled about, putting the porridge into a bowl for all to dip into and drawing a bench up to the table.

John laid out the little harp, put bread into his pouch, and stuck a knife in his belt. "I am no warrior," he said to Robin. "I am but a messenger and minstrel. But who knows? I might find myself close to the enemy. Closer than I would like," he added with a shrug.

The meal was soon over, and they made ready to start.

"Think you I can go so far again this day?" asked Robin anxiously.

"Thou hast no need to think of that," John assured him. "I can carry thee right well, as the good friar did. The harp and the crutches we shall strap on so they will not cumber us." He fastened the crutches to his side and the harp around Robin's neck, so it hung down his back. "Soon thou'lt be carrying thine own harp, God willing.

"Fare thee well, old Mother," said John, embracing her. "Up, now, young master," he said to Robin, and with that they left the cottage and went on their way.

"How shall we go?" asked Robin, as John strode down the path on the way out of the village. "Shall we go by the way I came here? Or by way of Letham Bridge?"

"Neither," answered John-go-in-the-Wynd. "I know still another way. I know a path leading through the forest to the southeast. It goeth past the priory where we shall ford the river. We can come at the town easily from there. Then we can wait for nightfall, and indeed it will be nightfall ere we arrive, but there will be a moon.

"We shall creep along the river, under cover of the reeds and willows, and enter the town through the shoemaker's house, which is on the wall. He is known to me, and we have a signal between us. He knoweth the sound of my harp, and the certain tune I play will tell him we have need of him. From there it is quite simple to get into the graveyard of the church, thence into the church itself, and into the tower. There we shall see all and hear all if we are not deafened by the bells."

"What an adventure to tell my father!" cried Robin.

Although he carried Robin, John trotted along at a good speed, for he knew every curve in the path. It was only a short way to the ford of the river, near the priory, and from there across fields covered with grazing sheep to the forest. There they rested. When they reached the top of the hill beyond, John pointed out the drovers' road far below. There, glints of light on lance and pennant, helmet, and moving figures showed Robin the fast-moving company of soldiers. Because it was nearly dusk and suppertime, blue smoke rose from every chimney pot in the village they had left, and in the low places mist began to rise.

"We must make haste," said John, lifting Robin again to his back, "or we shall be too late."

When they had to cross open country again, John kept to the hedgerows so they would not be seen, and as they came nearer to Lindsay, he kept well away from every barn and outbuilding.

"For aught we know the Welsh may be encamped out here on this side of the castle as well as on the other," he explained. "They might question even a minstrel such as I. 'Tis safer for our skins to go softly."

By the time they reached the place where the drovers' road led, John halted before crossing the road to observe the sentry. They waited for the sound of his footsteps to die away around the town. The moon was high, and by keeping well in the shadow of a tree they were able to cross the road without being seen.

"Ah," said John with a sigh of relief. "So far we have come safely. Soon Sir Hugh's men will encircle the town. By then we shall be in the church tower to give the signal for attack."

"We have not seen the enemy on this side of the town," whispered Robin hopefully.

"No," agreed John. "Because they have taken the town, and will be inside the walls. There is more need of outposts to the south and west, where the two bridges are, and where the roads leading from them are well traveled. The Welsh will reason that there is little likelihood of danger from this road because it is well known that Sir Peter and his cousin Sir Hugh are not on friendly terms. Sir Peter is for the King and for England. Sir Hugh is not. But they are of one family, and were once like brothers. I had little difficulty in persuading him. Sir Hugh."

"Perhaps they will be friends from now on," said Robin. "Perhaps Sir Hugh will be won for the King."

"It may be." John nodded. "Most of the lords in this part of the country are for keeping their lands to themselves. But times are changing, and we have a good king."

"Hark!" whispered Robin again. "All is still. The sentry is at the far end of his walk. Shall we go then?"

"Aye, 'tis time," said John. "Hast the little harp safe?"

"'Tis safe," said Robin, grasping John about the neck and getting himself settled on his back.

They crept forward again, shielded by the darkness, and made their way along a narrow path that followed the wall until the rising ground told John they were near to the shoemaker's cottage. There again they halted, to make sure no sentry was about. John, letting Robin slip to the ground, fitted the crutches under his arms and took the harp from about his neck.

The tune he layed was mournful and slow, but it must have reached the ears of the shoemaker. John was just beginning to play it for the third time when there was an answer to it in the form of a bagpipe jig. Robin could see John bobbing his head up and down happily because his playing had brought forth the right response. There followed

another period of waiting while the sentry passed again on the wall. They scarcely breathed until he had turned again and was going the other way. By counting his steps they knew when he was far enough away for them to act.

Then, without warning, a sort of chair was let down from the window high in the wall. John fastened Robin into it and gave the rope a jerk. Robin was hauled aloft so quickly that he had no time to think what he should do or what he should say. He found himself being lifted inside the upper room of a small house and the window drawn to. He faced a little man, who cautioned him to silence while again they waited for the sentry to come and to go.

There was no light in the room except the moonlight that came in through the window.

"This is really exciting," thought Robin.

He wished that John had been able to come into the house with him.

He heard the "tramp, tramp" of the sentry and the thudding of the pikestaff as it struck the stone when the sentry turned at the wall of the house. The sound lessened, and once more the rope was lowered.

This time it was for John. Robin could see the iron wheel under the window which turned like a windlass to let out the rope.

In a moment John stood in the room with him. The rope and iron wheel were stored in an innocent-looking chest. The shoemaker quickly lifted the wheel out of the strong wooden block which held it covered with a flat board and cloth. The shoemaker motioned for Robin and 145

John to follow him down the steep stair leading to the house below.

They did not linger in the house, but with a few words to the shoe-maker, left by way of the garden. There was a door in the wall leading into the graveyard of the church, where John and Robin slipped quietly from one great tombstone to another. They entered the church by the sanctuary door, startling the sacristan who slept and ate in a small room off the entrance porch.

"Who art thou?" he called, hearing the creak of the door. "Art friend or foe?"

"Hist!" warned John, stepping quickly toward the light of the lantern held by the sacristan. "We are friends. I am John-go-in-the-Wynd, minstrel. This lad is young Master Robin, friend and ward of Sir Peter. He hath this day saved us all." The sacristan held the lantern up where he could see John's face.

"Now I mind thee," he said, nodding his head. "I knew thy father."

John told the sacristan how Robin had come to warn him and to get help, and described the plan he had made with Sir Hugh to sound the bells giving the signal for attack.

"Come with me, then," said the sacristan, leading the way.

They went down the long, dark aisle of the church to the door of the tower.

"Give me thy crutches here, young master," said John. "Canst thou climb the ladder or wilt go pickaback? 'Tis a great height, but there are resting places."

"I can do it," said Robin shortly. Had he not climbed to the towers and turrets of the castle many times?

They had just reached the belfry when it was time for curfew to ring. The bells began an ear-splitting clamor.

"Down flat, and cover thy ears—quick!" shouted John.

They flattened themselves on the platform and endured the deafening sound.

"We shall go to the top first," said John, "for it is yet too soon to give the signal, and from there we shall see somewhat."

From the belfry to the top of the tower it was another thirty feet of climbing. When they reached the top Robin fell in a heap onto the platform with every bit of strength gone from his legs and arms. It slowly returned. In a little while he was able to rise and stand beside John, looking out over the town.

"We agreed that I should wait an hour after curfew, when the moon will be nearly overhead," said John. "That allows time for all companies to be in place, and with the sounding of the bell to move in about the town and castle wall at once."

"How can you tell when it has been an hour?" asked Robin.

"By the feel of it," said John. "Besides, I shall play 'Love a Garland Is' and 'Lament of a Lass.' That will be half of the hour." He unslung the harp from Robin's back and began the music.

While they waited for the rest of the hour to pass, John pointed out the familiar turrets of the castle, the north tower where they had stood that day, and the tower of the keep where the household waited for deliverance. He strummed on the harp between times.

They tried to see into the hills about the town, but saw only the quiet countryside bathed in moonlight. In the town, supper fires sent up blue smoke, and here and there was the red glare of torchlight and campfire. Glints of moonlight on helmet or shield shone from the walls where sentries walked, but very little sound could be heard at that height.

The hour was up.

"Now," said John, "it is time for the alarm. Stay thou here, and I shall return. Cover thy ears well, but watch to see what happens." He was gone through the hatch into the darkness below. Robin waited, his skin prickling with excitement. Would the signal be at the right time? Would the arrows find their mark and lift the siege?

Bong! BONGGG! BONGGG! BONGGG! BONG! BONGGG!!!!

The great bell rang, sending waves of sound that went out over the hills and came echoing back into the stone of the bell tower, which trembled with the vibration.

At first Robin could see nothing different from what he had seen before. Then, it was as if a part of the landscape itself moved off there toward the south, just below the edge of the town. Gathering from the slopes were tiny moving figures, now in the open, now lost in shadow.

Robin searched for another sign, this time in the direction of   **147**

Letham Bridge. The sign was there where he could see more clearly.

John came up, breathing hard.

"What's to be seen?" he asked. "Are they moving? Hast seen any arrows fly?" He looked to the Letham Bridge.

Then it came.

A hail of arrows that were like dark rain sped from oncoming yeomen, dropping the sentries on the bridge and picking off men of the guard manning the wall of the town. From where they stood Robin could see it all as plainly as if it had been a toy village set in a toy landscape, and the soldiers, toy soldiers. He saw pikemen strike down sentries of the enemy at the town gate and take prisoner the Welsh guards. He saw the company of Sir Hugh's men enter and take the town.

It had been a complete surprise.

When John-go-in-the-Wynd saw what was happening and realized that the plan had been successful, he tossed his hat into the air and clasped Robin in his arms.

"We've won!" he shouted. "The Welsh are routed! Lindsay is saved once more!"

Then, setting Robin on his feet again, he said,

"Stay thou here, and watch how the Welsh are marched out of the town whilst I go below. Thou'lt hear such a peal of bells as shall nigh wake the dead lying below." Down he went again through the hatch to the belfry.

With the pealing of the bells, flares went up from castle and town, windows and doors opened. The peal of bells stopped. John came back and together they watched the lifting of the siege. They could see people running about through the street embracing one another, tossing caps and hats into the air, and in other ways showing their joy at being freed from the Welsh invaders. In a short while they saw the enemy marched out of town.

Tears streamed down Robin's cheeks.

"I must not cry," he thought, wiping them away. "Not even for joy."

"Now," said John, lifting Robin aloft, "thou'lt be carried on my shoulder—so. For thou'rt the hero of this victory," and together they

went down the long stretches of ladder and stair to the ground.

"Make haste," said Robin. "Let us go to the keep at once, so Sir Peter and Lady Constance shall know that I am safe and well. Brother Luke will be sure of it, for his prayers have followed me this day. That I know."

All the way through the town square John made his way with Robin on his shoulder high above the villagers dancing in the dawn of returning day.

They were greeted with cheers at the castle gate and followed across the courtyard to the inner gate and to the keep by the cheering crowd.

Alan-at-Gate saw them from the gatehouse. The drawbridge was lowered and the portcullis raised, and just inside the whole company of the household stood to receive them. Sir Peter was in the center with his sons and the two pages. Near him was Lady Constance with her women and little Alison. D'Ath whimpered joyfully beside Brother Luke.

Sir Peter held out his arms and helped Robin to the ground, placing the crutches to support him. Then, placing his hand upon Robin's head, he spoke solemnly.

"Now, before God and this company," he said, "I do hail thee Conqueror and true son of thy noble father."

Lady Constance embraced Robin and the women made much of him. D'Ath was too well bred a dog to push himself forward, but his eager prancing and wriggling finally brought him to Robin's side, where he thrust his long, cold nose into Robin's hands.

Sea Fever

JOHN MASEFIELD

Illustrated by Wesley Dennis

I must go down to the seas again,
   to the lonely sea and the sky,
And all I ask is a tall ship
   and a star to steer her by,
And the wheel's kick and the wind's song
   and the white sail's shaking
And a gray mist on the sea's face,
   and a gray dawn breaking.

I must go down to the seas again,
   for the call of the running tide
Is a wild call and a clear call
   that may not be denied;
And all I ask is a windy day
   with the white clouds flying,
And the flung spray and the blown spume,
   and the sea gulls crying.

I must go down to the seas again,
   to the vagrant gypsy life,
To the gull's way and the whale's way
   where the wind's like a whetted knife;
And all I ask is a merry yarn
   from a laughing fellow-rover,
And quiet sleep and a sweet dream
   when the long trick's over.

The Sun

BY JOHN DRINKWATER

Illustrated by Helen Prickett

I told the Sun that I was glad,
   I'm sure I don't know why;
Somehow the pleasant way he had
   Of shining in the sky,
Just put a notion in my head
   That wouldn't it be fun
If, walking on the hill, I said
   "I'm happy" to the Sun.

A Cheese for Lafayette

BY ELISABETH MEG

Illustrated by Helen Belkin

The American War for Independence was over. The brave
young French nobleman, the Marquis de Lafayette,
had helped George Washington and the American patriots
win it. But now little Nantucket Island was in trouble,
and again the generous young Frenchman helped his
American friends. How could the people of Nantucket
thank him? They found a way that will make you laugh
and be proud, too, as you read this story.

ONCE UPON A TIME, long ago, the good people of Nantucket
were worried. Usually, they were not the worrying kind. They were
rich and happy. They owned the loveliest island in the world, where
they lived in snug little gray houses beside their sheltered harbors.

They had bought their island from the Indians, for £30 sterling
and two beaver hats. And it was a great bargain!

Their island was always beautiful, white in a gray sea in winter,
green in a blue sea in summer. It had moorlands of wild roses and
sweet fern and buttercups. It had fields of huckleberries which the
barefoot island children loved to pick in July. It had marshy pastures
of salt grass and sandy pastures of bent grass where the fat cows grazed.
It had fresh-water fish in its little blue ponds and salt-water fish in
its big ocean. And it had whales!

The whales were the most important of all, because oil came from
the whales. And in those days, when there were no electric lights,
everybody needed oil to make candles of, or to burn in their lamps.

The people of Nantucket sent out their whaling ships to bring
home the whale oil. They put the oil into barrels, and sent it to mar-
kets over the sea. They sold the oil for money, and used the money to

153

buy shoes and cotton cloth and meat and flour and other things for comfortable living. The people of Nantucket had everything they needed in those days.

The whales gave them something else, too. They gave them adventure! On the quiet little island, there were not many amusements. But when the whaling ships came in, and all the men were home again, the people would gather for a great dinner that was like a feast. All the best of the good island food would be set out on the long tables. Afterward, everyone would sit about and listen to stories of the sea, tales of danger and daring. The Nantucket people would not have exchanged one of these island evenings for the gayest dancing party on the mainland.

But all that was in the happy days, before the Nantucket people were worried. Now a big war had come, and war always brings trouble. People get angry and do spiteful, selfish things. So the people over the sea, who used to buy the whale oil, said, "We don't like you any more and won't buy your whale oil! We'd rather do without!" As if that weren't bad enough, most of the whaling ships were sunk in the war.

"We could build new ships," said the people of Nantucket, "but if nobody will buy our oil, what's the use?"

So they had no adventure stories and no money, and it is little wonder that the people of Nantucket were worried.

"What shall we do?" everyone was asking his neighbor. "Our shoes are wearing out, our coats are ragged, there is no flour left in our flour bins. What shall we do?"

But suddenly one day the town bell ringer began ringing his bell like mad, and all of the people ran out of their houses to see what was the matter. The men ran, the women ran, the children ran. Stout John Massey, the shipbuilder, and Friend Thompson with his seven boys and girls, and hobbly old Granny Willis, and Prudence Jennet with her little daughter Abigail, and all the others came running down the street and into the market place.

"Good news!" cried Thomas Quig, the moderator, waving a big white envelope in his hand. "Good news!"

154   "What is it? What?" asked everybody at once.

"Lafayette—" began Thomas Quig.

"Who is Lafayette?" whispered the tallest Thompson boy to his father.

"You remember, the great Frenchman—George Washington's friend. He helped us win the war—"

"The Marquis de Lafayette," boomed Thomas Quig in a loud voice, "has talked to the King of France—"

Everybody began to mumble, "What good is that? What does the King care about Nantucket?"

"Peace, neighbors!" cried Thomas Quig. "How can I tell you the news in such a babble?"

Everyone was quiet.

"The King has promised that the French people will buy our oil. We will build new ships, and with someone to buy our oil, we shall soon be rich again."

The people of Nantucket were sober people. They did not throw up their hats and shout "hurray!" Instead, they thought this over gravely. At last, Friend Thompson smiled a big smile and said warmly, "This is a good thing. This man Lafayette is indeed a friend to us."

"We owe him much," came the gentle voice of Prudence Jennet. "We must thank him kindly for this good deed."

"Yes," agreed everyone, "we must write him a nice polite letter from us all."

Granny Willis pounded on a barrelhead with her cane, and everyone was quiet.

"A letter is not enough! We should send him a present."

That seemed a good idea, until John Massey said, "What have we poor folk of Nantucket to send to

a rich man like that? He lives in a palace and wears fine lace on his velvet coat, and no doubt he has bags of money besides."

"Just the same, we should send him a present," insisted Granny, and since nobody said anything, she added, "I could weave him a good woolen coverlet from my own sheep. Even rich folks need to keep warm at night."

"No," said Thomas Quig slowly, "that won't do. Nothing could be finer than one of Granny's woolen coverlets, but that would be from Granny, and this present must be from all of us. Everyone must give something."

There wasn't a sound in the market place for almost five minutes. The people of Nantucket were thinking. Then up piped the shy little voice of Abigail Jennet.

"Has thee thought of a cheese?" she asked, and then added, all in a rush, "Our own good cheese! There is none better in the world, they say. Our whalers carry it on their voyages, and far from home our men enjoy it, and think of our marshy meadows and our four windmills with their arms turning and our island cows coming home at sundown to be milked and the sound of new milk in the milk pails. Often I've heard them tell it!"

She stopped, out of breath. She had never before in her life said so much at one time. Her neighbors looked at her in amazement. Then everybody began to talk at once.

"A cheese!"

"The very thing!"

"Frenchmen are said to like cheese—"

"And cheese would keep well on a long voyage."

"It should be a big one, the finest we've ever made on the island—"

At last the bell ringer had to ring the bell to bring the talking to an end.

"It has been agreed," said Thomas Quig, "that the people of Nantucket will send a cheese to Lafayette. Now there are five hundred households on our island, and every family has a cow. If tomorrow each household will give a night's milking, and the next day a morning's milking, we should have enough for a very fine cheese."

156   "Yes! Yes!" cried everyone. "We will! We will!" and the people,

talking excitedly about the good news and the cheese, went back to their little gray houses.

The next day was like a holiday. People looked out of doors and leaned over fences to see the cows led out to pasture by the town shepherd. Some of the little boys tagged along, and spent the day leading Daisy or Dinglebell to especially juicy clumps of grass. In the afternoon, some of the girls went too. At sundown, when the cows came home, they were garlanded with posies as for a parade.

Every family stood that night to watch its cow being milked; it seemed that never before had the island cows given so much milk or so rich. The milk was poured into barrels, and from the barrels into the cheesemaker's tub. The next day, the morning milk was added, and now the cheese for Lafayette was begun.

It takes a long time to make a cheese. It also takes much care and skill. The wisest dairy woman in Nantucket was chosen to oversee this task. She knew just how warm the milk must be, and how much rennet would be needed to thicken it. After she had stirred in the rennet with a big paddle, she floated a wooden bowl on top of the milk, and stood watching with sharp eyes while the milk "set," as junket does.

When the milk was so firm that the bowl could be lifted out clean, and leave a little hollow in the curd, she called other women to help her. With long cheese knives they cut the curd into big squares, then into smaller squares. The whey, almost as clear as water, began to separate from the curd, and the women with their wooden whey bowls dipped and dipped. Then they broke the curd into even smaller pieces, and worked it with their hands. Still more whey came out.

The carpenter had made an enormous cheese mold out of strong oak. It was like a wooden tub, with holes bored in the bottom, and it had a loose lid that could be pushed down on top of the cheese.

The women lined the cheese mold with calico cloth, and the men packed the curd into it. They piled the curd high in the middle, so that the press could push it down into every curve of the mold. They wanted no holes or ragged edges in this cheese for Lafayette!

Into the press went the curd in its mold; out flew the whey through the holes in the bottom. The men pressed and turned and pressed again. Now they turned it out of the mold and onto a fresh piece of

calico cloth. What magic! The curd had turned into a cheese. And what a beautiful, yellow, full moon of a cheese it was!

Still it was not finished. It went back to the press, and there it stayed all night, while the cheesemakers got a good night's rest. In the morning it was pressed for the last time. Now a light wooden hoop was fitted around it, so that its edges would not chip off, and it was rolled into the salting room. For five days it was turned every day, and rubbed with salt to give it a fine salty tang. Then it was painted with Indian red to preserve it, and now it was handsomer than ever.

Half the town came to see it weighed.

The housewives came, with babies in their arms and little children holding to their skirts. The older children came from school with their schoolmaster. The coopers left their barrel making; the smiths left their forges; the calkers and the carpenters left their work on the ships. The whaling men home from the sea came, too, and the ship chandler watched from the door of his shop. Even a few shy Indians stood at the edge of the crowd, curious to know what the commotion was about. There was a buzz of excitement.

Five hundred pounds! Who had ever heard of such a cheese! Everyone in Nantucket was bursting with pride.

The great cheese was rolled into the ripening loft, and there it lay for many months, being turned with loving care every few days, so that the ripening would be perfect.

At last it was finished, packed, and ready for its long voyage. Everyone came down to the wharf to see it off. Friend Jonas, the schoolmaster, had painted the address on the side of the box. He used his fanciest lettering, full of flourishes and bold and black.

The Marquis de Lafayette

Château de Chavaniac

Auvergne,

France.

"Chavaniac—that's the palace where he lives," said one.

"I hear that he has a pretty wife and three children, a son and two little daughters," said another.

"And did you know," asked the schoolmaster, "that his son is named for our own General Washington? George Washington Lafayette, that boy is called."

"George Washington Lafayette," repeated little Abigail Jennet, "I hope *he* likes cheese!"

"Anyhow, it's the biggest cheese in the world," said Friend Thompson's youngest boy, "and I wish I could see Mistress Lafayette's eyes pop open when it rolls in through the door of her old palace!"

With shouting and tugging, the cheese was rolled up the gangplank and let down into the hold of the ship.

The sailors shouted, the people cheered. The anchor chains clanked and the ropes whined.

The people stood watching until the ship had weighed anchor and sailed with full white sails out of the harbor. Then many climbed to the roof walks of their houses, and watched until it disappeared beyond the horizon.

And every one of them was saying proudly in his heart, "From the people of Nantucket—a cheese for Lafayette!"

"And did Lafayette like it," you ask, "and was his wife really surprised?"

Indeed, when the Marquise de Lafayette saw it, she cried in dismay, "*Mon dieu!* Whatever shall we do with such a monster of a cheese?"

But when the servants had uncrated it, and the chef had cut out the first rich, fragrant slice, she knew exactly what to do. She would share it.

She sent part of it to Paris, to their house in the rue de Bourbon, to be served at the big parties there. She sent pieces of it to all their friends and relations, and to all the servants in the town house, and to all the peasants on the estate at Chavaniac. She sent a piece to the village school, for a treat, and another to the curé for his poor people. And to all she said proudly, "With the compliments of the Marquis. It was sent to him by admirers in America."

The children said, between bites, "How many mice would it take how many years to eat up five hundred pounds of cheese? And please, *maman*, may we have another piece?"

Everyone who knew the Lafayettes was eating cheese, and saying to each other, "It is surprisingly good for a foreign cheese. Of course, there is nothing quite like French cheese, but this Nantucket cheese is really very good."

And the great Lafayette himself, how did he like it?

Because he had a warm heart and dearly loved plain people, you can be sure that he never had a gift in all his life, not his golden sword, nor his medals, nor all his honors, that pleased and touched him more than the big cheese from the good people of Nantucket.

Navaho Friend

BY EVELYN SIBLEY LAMPMAN

Illustrated by Paul Lantz

Once Rose had been called Sad Girl. That was when she
lived with her grandmother on the Navaho Reservation.
Now Rose was at the Chemawa Indian School in
Oregon, and a happy new life had opened for her. How
she learned a wonderful secret of friendship makes
an exciting story of an Indian girl of today.

ROSE ALWAYS fell asleep quickly once she climbed into her bed,
but one night she was awakened with a start. The room was en-
shrouded in thick blackness, and because there was no moon the open
window was a square of dark gray, only a little lighter in shade.

She had been aroused by a sound, a strange muffled sound which
seemed to come from far away, and at first she clutched the bed-
clothes tightly, almost afraid to breathe. It could very well be the
ghost of an earth person, for everyone knows that ghosts appear only
after darkness, and on moonless nights. Then she realized it wasn't the
mourning voice of a ghost, for the sound was not from outside. It was
in the room, and it came from the bed below her own. Isobel was
making that strange muffled noise. She was crying.

Rose leaned over the edge of the bunk.

"Isobel!" she whispered. "Isobel, what's the matter?"

Isobel did not answer, but for a moment the crying stopped. Then
it started again, as though it was beyond her control.

Rose swung her feet over the edge and slipped to the floor. It
would be just as well not to awaken the peacefully sleeping twins.
She sat on the edge of Isobel's bed and reached over to pat the shaking shoulders.

"Isobel, has a sickness taken hold of you? Shall I call the matron?" 161

Isobel's whole body shook in protest. It announced that she was not sick. She didn't want the matron.

Rose didn't feel that the matron would do much good either. If Isobel had contracted sickness or disease it was because she had violated a taboo or had been attacked by a ghost or a witch .If the latter was the case and the spectral attack was very recent it could be averted or lessened by certain precautions.

She fumbled her way through the darkness to the dresser. Her fingers slipped down, counting, until they arrived at her own drawer. Inside, carefully laid away with her change of underwear and her sweater, was a tiny sack of gall medicine. Grandmother had made it for her just before she left home, so it was fresh and potent. It was composed of dried and pulverized galls of many animals and was a sure cure for anyone who had unknowingly absorbed a witch's poison.

"Get up, Isobel," Rose insisted in a firm whisper. "You've got to come with me."

The bed once more shook with Isobel's refusal.

Rose pulled back the blankets firmly, holding them there despite Isobel's fumbling attempts to jerk them back. One of the twins moved restlessly and mumbled something in her sleep.

"If you don't come, I'll wake Dolores and Maria. Three of us can drag you," whispered Rose fiercely.

Isobel got out of bed. Her crying was not so violent as before, but her sturdy body shook with an occasional racking sob. Rose took her by the hand, guiding her out of the room. A dim light was kept burning at night in the long corridor, and Isobel's face appeared red and puffy. She must have been crying a long time before I heard her, Rose told herself anxiously. She hoped it was not too late for the gall medicine to take effect. There was only one cure for the poison of a witch or a ghost, once it had really taken hold, and that was to have the Enemy Way sung over the victim. No one here would know or be qualified to perform such a ceremonial.

She pulled Isobel into the deserted bathroom, switched on the light, and closed the door firmly behind them. Fortunately someone had left a water glass on the shelf, and she filled it at the tap, dumping in a generous sprinkling of gall medicine from the bag. She knew

it should be boiled a long while to produce the necessary qualities of an emetic, but there was no time for that. Isobel's swollen red face showed she was already too far gone to wait.

"Drink it," she ordered sternly, holding out the glass.

Isobel accepted it meekly. Tonight she had lost all of her former disdainful manner. She looked very forlorn and pitiful. Her shoulders, in the outing-flannel sleeves of her pajamas, sagged mournfully, and already she seemed to be coming down with a chill.

"It's gall medicine," explained Rose. "My grandmother made it for me. Drink it fast."

Isobel obeyed. The water, choked with shriveled brown fragments, disappeared down her throat. She shuddered a little, gulped, and held out the empty glass.

"You'll feel better soon," promised Rose, trying to make her voice carry an assurance she did not feel. "We'll go back to bed soon, and in the morning you'll feel fine."

"No," said Isobel in a choked voice. "I won't. I know I won't."

But she had stopped crying, which was a good sign. Perhaps it was not too late for the gall medicine to work after all. Rose waited, while they both shivered with cold, for the emetic to take effect. Nothing happened, and finally they gave up. There was no use waiting any longer.

They tiptoed back down the murky corridor and into their own room where the twins continued to sleep peacefully. Isobel climbed into bed, and, without thinking, Rose leaned over and tucked the sheepskins around her. Grandmother always tucked the sheepskins around Rose when she was sad or upset, and it seemed a natural thing to do. In the darkness she heard Isobel catch her breath. There was a little pause before she whispered a weak good night.

"Good night," answered Rose. She tried very hard to sound bright and reassuring. "I'll see you in the morning."

In the morning, however, Isobel was not in her bed. She must have got up and dressed while it was still night. Her pajamas were thrown on the floor, and most amazing of all, the bed itself was tumbled and unmade.

"Where's Isobel?" demanded Dolores.

"She probably went down the hall," answered Maria carelessly.

Rose said nothing, but she was troubled about their roommate's absence. After she had finished making her own bed, she made Isobel's, and hung the two pairs of pajamas in the closet. The gall medicine had been taken too late. Isobel's body was already filled with the witch's poison. But where was she? Even though ill and filled with poison she still had to be somewhere.

There was no sign of her at breakfast, nor did she appear in the classroom when school took up. Mrs. Hughes called the roll, and each pupil except Isobel answered "present" to his name.

"Is Isobel sick?" asked Mrs. Hughes of Miss Fox.

Miss Fox shook her head and inquired of the class.

"Do any of you girls know what has happened to Isobel?"

Everyone looked blank, and after a moment Rose put up her hand. She couldn't keep the secret any longer. Isobel must be found and sent home. She must return to the reservation so that the proper singers could perform the Enemy Way ceremonial.

"May I speak to you, Miss Fox? May I speak to you alone?"

Miss Fox looked startled and said something to Mrs. Hughes. Then she beckoned Rose to follow her out of the room and into the hall.

"Tell me what has happened," she insisted as the door closed behind them.

Rose told the whole story of waking up and discovering there was

no moon, of hearing Isobel's sobs, and her own realization that a ghost or a witch was abroad in the night. She told of the gall medicine, and how it hadn't worked properly because it hadn't been boiled, and how in the morning she had discovered that Isobel had been spirited away.

Miss Fox listened carefully to everything.

"Rose," she said finally. "It was not a witch or a ghost who poisoned Isobel. There are no ghosts or witches here. Isobel is sick from something else. She is sick with loneliness."

"With loneliness?"

"She has never been away from home before," nodded Miss Fox. "I know that the rest of you haven't either, but people are made differently inside. They have different feelings and express those feelings differently. You have had moments of homesickness when you thought of your family and wished you were with them. But those moments have passed because you have made other friends and have found things to occupy your mind. You have kept busy and are adjusting to your surroundings. I have watched Isobel for some time, and I've been worried about her. She doesn't seem to have any special friends. I always see her alone."

"She doesn't want to make friends, Miss Fox."

"How do you know she doesn't? Did she tell you so?"

"No, but she doesn't act friendly. She acts as though she thought she was better than anyone else. She never says anything to anybody. I know she doesn't, because she lives in the same room with me. She doesn't talk. She doesn't even look at us very much. She wants to be by herself."

"Do you know what it is to be shy, Rose?"

Shy? She, who once was called Sad Girl because she kept to herself and never smiled? Rose almost laughed aloud, but Miss Fox was looking too serious to dare such a thing.

"She isn't shy, Miss Fox. Why should she be shy? What does she have to be shy about?"

"I don't know that any more than you do. But I know she is. Think back, Rose. You say that Isobel has never given any sign that she wanted to be friends. Have you ever given her a sign that you'd like to be her friend?"

Rose hung her head. There was much in what Miss Fox said. The friends she herself had made since leaving home had all of them given her to understand they were willing to be friendly. There was Lucy on the bus, Miss Fox and the teachers, Cora Mae and many of the boys and girls in her class. There was Mary Yucca at home. Grace and Tony would have been friendly if only she had let them.

She realized suddenly that it had always been the other person who gave the first signal of friendship, the smile, the word or gesture. She herself had never volunteered such a thing. She didn't exactly know how to go about it. Perhaps Isobel didn't know either.

"I'm going to explain things to Mrs. Hughes, then I'm going to look for Isobel." Miss Fox was watching her closely. "You may return to class, Rose, or you may be excused to go with me. It's up to you to decide."

"I'll go with you to find Isobel."

Miss Fox smiled, showing both dimples. She went back to speak with Mrs. Hughes, and Rose waited in the hall. She tried to think where they should look first. Isobel couldn't be in their own dormitory. Someone had been in every part of that earlier in the morning. Unless Isobel had played hide-and-seek she would have been discovered before this. The same thing was true of the other dormitories, the classrooms and administration buildings. She must be outside.

Rose closed her eyes to think better. The grounds at Chemawa were quite open, and for some reason she doubted if Isobel would be hiding in the shrubbery. Probably she had gone off the grounds. She might be walking home along the highway, or perhaps she had wandered onto one of the neighboring farms. A farm! That was it. Some place that smelled faintly of home, where there was no one around, and where she could imagine she was back in her native Utah.

"Gracious," said Miss Fox in dismay when Rose told her of her conclusions. "You may be right, but that covers a lot of territory. There are acres of farm lands adjoining the school property."

"But I think I know where to look," insisted Rose eagerly. "The day we went to the State Fair we saw one place where there were sheep. We saw them from the bus windows. Everyone spoke of them. It was like seeing home, and we wished they were closer to the road. I think if I were Isobel and homesick I would remember the sheep and go there."

"Very well," agreed Miss Fox. "We'll look there first. Show me the place of the sheep."

The scents of fall were beginning to fill the air, and its colors marked the countryside with splotches of yellow and red. Someone was burning trash, and a tinge of smoke hung low over the fields. The sky had lost its vivid summer shade and looked faded. Blue always did that eventually, Rose told herself. She remembered a bolt of bright blue velveteen on the trader's shelf at Goose Hollow. Everyone admired it, but no one could afford to buy it. They chose scarlets and crimsons when they were buying material for new blouses. Reds would keep their colors through many years, but under the blazing reservation sun a blue would soon fade to light, then an ugly gray. It would take a very rich woman indeed to afford a sky-colored blouse which would soon lose its color.

They walked down the gravel road which led to the highway, and Rose pointed out the field where they had glimpsed the sheep.

"There were only a few," she remembered, "and it is not a large field. Perhaps by now they have moved on to another pasture."

"We'll look, anyway," decided Miss Fox. She left the road and struck off across the rough, grassy field. "There's a fence line over there. They keep sheep fenced in this part of the country. If they're still pastured here it will be in an enclosure."

Rose thought how strange it was to fence grazing land. Sheep took 167 a lot of pasture. They had to wander miles in order to find forage. Then she looked at the countryside through which they were walking and realized that what held true at home was not so in this place. Here the grass grew thick, covering the soil completely—not in scattered clumps. The duties of a herder would be small, for there was no sagebrush to make the greedy sheep puff up should they eat it, no locoweed to make them run in senseless circles. She wondered what white childrens did to occupy their time since they were not needed to tend the flocks.

They reached the fence, and Miss Fox parted the strands of wire, holding up the top which was barbed with sharp spikes. Rose climbed through, then held it for Miss Fox. They were in a field where the sheep had been, but there was no sign of them now.

"We'll walk a little way farther," decided Miss Fox. "If you remember this place, Isobel may remember it too."

A hundred yards on they found her. Isobel was sitting on the ground as she had so often sat on her own bed in the dormitory, her hands clasped on her lap, her knees folded under her. She had been screened from sight by the slope of the land, but when she saw them coming she made no move to run away. She did not speak or wave a greeting, and her face wore an expression of hopelessness.

Miss Fox said nothing either. She sat on the ground beside Isobel, and after a moment Rose sat on the other side. For a long time they were silent, and Rose felt a sense of companionship gradually come over her. It was the same feeling she and Grandmother had often shared at night in the hogan. They said nothing, but after a while it seemed that speech was unnecessary, for their thoughts were shared.

"It is good to sit here," said Isobel after a long time. "There has been no one around me but the Holy People. Changing Woman, the earth, is preparing for her old age which comes with the winter. I do not think she minds that she must grow old for a time, for she knows she will be young again in the spring. I saw Dawn Boy in the sky early this morning, and now Sun, the husband of Changing Woman, smiles at me. Gila Monster also knows I am here, for he has sent some soft winds from the south to blow upon me."

"It is good to be with old friends," said Miss Fox softly. "But new friends are good, too."

"I have no new friends." Isobel's voice was steady. Her tears had run dry the night before. "This is not a good place for me. There is no happiness here. The others here do not like me, but at home I am liked. I have many friends at home. It is better that I go home, Miss Fox. I should not have come."

"Isobel, you're wrong. You do have friends here. I am your friend," cried Rose. She found that she was telling the truth. This was a new Isobel who sat beside her on the grass. This one wasn't proud and disdainful at all. Even her turquoise and silver jewelry meant nothing today. They represented the "hard" wealth of a Navaho, but one can have more than his share of "hard" wealth and still be poor. He is poor if he is without songs and stories and without friends.

Isobel turned and looked at her steadily after Rose spoke, and then she smiled a little wistfully. Rose realized with surprise that Isobel was pretty when she smiled. It made her seem a different person.

"Thank you," she said gravely. "You are kind. You tried to be kind last night. You are kind today. But I must go home."

"It will be different if you stay," pleaded Rose. "You don't know how different it will be. You'll have many friends. I'll ask Mrs. Hughes if you can change your seat to be by Cora Mae and me. You'll have your meals with us. And when the twins laugh and giggle with each other, you and I can share a little joke of our own."

Isobel looked doubtful.

"Will you try it for a week?" asked Miss Fox. "Will you give the school one more chance? I promise you that if you're still homesick after another week I'll help you go back home."

"I will try," agreed Isobel after another silence. "My family wanted me to come here, and I wanted to come. But they would want me to be happy."

"You will be happy," promised Rose quickly. "You're going to be very happy."

She got to her feet and reached a hand to pull Isobel to hers. Isobel looked surprised and smiled shyly as she accepted the offer. Somehow, as the three of them retraced their steps across the field, they found they were still clinging to each other's hands.

The Wooden Locket

BY ALICE ALISON LIDE *and* MARGARET ALISON JOHANSEN

Illustrated by Corydon Bell

What was the secret of the wooden locket? Jan Voda
treasured it carefully for he had brought the locket all
the way from Poland when he and his family came to seek
a new life of freedom in America. But it was hard
to be a stranger in a strange land. Even after
the Vodas settled on the Foster farm in the swamplands
of Alabama, there were troubles and misunderstandings.
How could Tilka, Jan's cousin, find courage to forget
the fears that had haunted her since the war? Could
Jan's wonderful secret gift from Poland help them
find happiness in this new land? You will find the heart-
warming answers as you read this story.

"OH, JAN," Tilka pleaded. "Help me think up something nice to
do for Mrs. Foster."

The boy wrinkled his brow in thought. "She likes flowers," he suggested. "You might work around the flowerbeds."

Tilka shook her head sadly. Mrs. Foster was forever digging and
watering, but the soil was too sandy for the plants to thrive.

A grin broke over Jan's face. Too sandy? What those flowerbeds
needed was a mulch of peat moss. And there was a peat moss deposit
not a hundred yards from where they talked. He had glimpsed it the
afternoon he had gone on to discover his island—he had meant to
come back and cut some, then had forgotten all about it.

"You come." Laughingly he pulled Tilka to her feet. "I show a something
your Mrs. Foster will like."

A little farther along the ridge Jan left Tilka on high ground while he eased down the slope to those flats of shallow water all overgrown with wild rosemary and leatherleaf. To his testing feet the water-covered ground felt spongy, yet firm enough for a support if one moved carefully. From beneath lush-growing bushes he scrabbled out, both hands full of peat moss—the stems and leaves of a swamp-growing moss that had rotted in the damp and, through the years, had been pressed down into a hard solid mass.

When Jan held the dripping stuff aloft, Tilka, as swamp-bred as he, shrieked delightedly. "The peat moss, him that makes the plants grow big, big!"

She wanted to rush right into harvesting the black muck, but Jan waved her back. "Tomorrow we come in the old clothes, start a real digging."

Tilka gave Jan's arm a happy squeeze. "Don't tell anybody," she begged. "Our secret, *nie?* We'll surprise Mrs. Foster."

After school the next day the two raced through their home jobs. Then they grabbed up a couple of spades and slipped away to the swamp.

Clearing a space by breaking away the brush, Jan stuck a spade into the soft ground to mark off a square, then lifted out a block of the dark slimy peat moss, and stepped back to put it up on the ridge.

Working beside him, Tilka began spading out the stuff too. They arranged their damp blocks in a neat row for drying. From muddy hands, smudges spread to nose, cheeks, and garments. After half an hour of cutting peat they looked as if they might have been rolling in the mud.

A twig slapped Tilka's face. She reached up a hand to break it out of the way, and something cold slid over her fingertips. Jerking back her hand, she stood frozen for an instant, staring into black, unwinking eyes.

"Snake—a snake!" Her scream rose high. Dropping the spade, she fled up the ridge. Jan raced behind her.

"What's the matter?" Philip popped up at the pasture gate. "Thought I heard yelling."

"A snake—there in the swamp," gasped Tilka, her eyes big with fright. "I almost had my hand on it."

The tall boy put on a superior air. "Of course there are snakes in the swamp. Hundreds of 'em. Thousands of 'em, I guess. Better stay away from the swamp if you don't want to get snake-bit."

Jan looked stubborn. "No snake's going to keep me out of the swamp."

Philip laughed. "So, Mister Hard-Head! Then it's up to me to give you some stuff to keep off the snakes. Come along to the tool shed, and I'll see what we can find."

As he led the way back to the yard, Philip explained that when the fruit trees were sprayed with lime-sulphur he'd noticed snakes leaving the orchard in every direction. Maybe snakes didn't like the sulphur smell. Anyhow, there was about half a quart can of lime-sulphur powder left over. They could use it, and he felt pretty certain the snakes would hurry to get out of their way.

Ugh, the stink of the stuff! But Jan and Tilka smeared it on their clothes and went bravely back to their work.

Every afternoon after school they would put on their old duds, perfume themselves with lime-sulphur, and quietly slip away to their peat-moss cutting.

Jan frowned as he stooped over the blocks they had laid out along the edge of the ridge. The moss wasn't drying as quickly as it should.

The place was too damp; open sunshine was needed for quick curing. But he'd hate the job of moving all the stuff to another spot.

Tilka read his thoughts. "Kos could pull it on the little sled," she said.

The few trials of the calf hitched to the sled hadn't been very successful. Kos needed weeks more of training before he'd be a real draft animal. But it wouldn't do any harm if the sled turned over. They could just pile the peat back again. And that would be a whole lot pleasanter than having to lug all the blocks in their hands.

So the light yoke of bent wood was put around the calf's neck, the rope was passed under his body and fastened to the sled, and Kos was led down the path toward the swamp. He stepped cautiously, looking wary, and snorting in loud suspicion of the strange sights and smells.

Tilka stroked the satiny neck. "Good Kos, good Kos," she soothed.

And Kos was good. He stood quietly while they piled the peat blocks on the sled, and didn't overturn a single load, though they had to make several trips to get all the blocks spread out in a sunny place.

Now that the peat moss was drying properly, Jan and Tilka could hardly wait till they could deliver their present to Mrs. Foster. First, though, they had to break up the blocks and shred the moss into a light fluffy mass. Then they had to take Papa Voda into their secret and get him to bring a huge cardboard box from the Trotter store.

Saturday morning a strange procession wound up the path from the swamp, through the pasture gate, and into the Foster back yard. First came Jan, leading Kos, who dragged the sled with its load of peat moss in the big cardboard box. Then Tilka, a hand on the box to keep it steady, was trailed by Josef and Binkie.

"Gracious me, what is all this?" Mrs. Foster appeared on the porch.

"For you—for your flowerbeds." Jan and Tilka spoke together. "Peat moss, from the swamp."

Mrs. Foster took a look in the box. "Well, I do declare, it is peat moss. And you got it from our very own swamp, when nobody else knew it was there!" She was patting Kos, hugging Tilka, smiling at Jan and small brother Josef. "You smart children! How can I ever thank you? This is the nicest thing anybody's done for me in a long time."

"We'll spread it out for you if you want us to," Tilka offered eagerly.

After pulling on her rubber gardening gloves, Mrs. Foster delightedly joined in the digging. And so did Betsy, squatting beside Tilka and happily telling the world, "Me help mine Tilka dig."

"Gosh, real peat moss from the swamp here!" Philip paused a moment in amazement, then hopped into the car to go on an errand with his father.

As the automobile swung down the lane, the motor back-fired with a sharp explosion like gunfire.

"Oh-oo—" Tilka bit back the exclamation of terror, steadied herself, went on with her work.

Watching the girl from the tail of her eye, Mrs. Foster nodded approvingly. Tilka was getting her fears under control.

While they worked, Jan told about things one saw in the swamp. "Lilies, iris, plants with leaves—oh, big, big!" The boy waved his arms grandly. "I could bring some of them all for your garden. You would like that, *nie?*"

"I would like that, *yes.*" Mrs. Foster laughed. "And you are just like my brother Bob, under the spell of the swamp magic. As a youngster, Bob was forever disappearing into the swamp. We lived pretty close by, over on the other side, but I was afraid of the swamp and wouldn't follow him very far in. Now Bob is a dignified lawyer in the city, but he still loves to work with plants. He's got a big greenhouse in his back yard. Someday I'll have to take you there to see his orchid collection."

Yes, Jan thought, the marshland has laid its magic spell on him.

Whenever he had an hour or two to himself he slipped away to the swamp on solitary excursions. Sometimes he followed animal trails along almost invisible ridges that threaded the muck. Sometimes he took the raft and poled down the dark water-runs, looking at the strange blossoms, listening to strange swamp sounds.

On his island Jan cleared a space in the tangled brush and made a garden of his own, transplanting bulbs and young seedlings from other sections of the swamp.

As he came again and again to work in his garden, the feeling grew in Jan that his island was not just any ordinary piece of high ground in the midst of a swamp, but that it possessed a secret hidden in its green depths. This feeling first came to him the day he pushed through the underbrush to where a double row of trees stood like a border to an avenue, and, in the narrow way between, only low, creeping plants were growing. Scratching about in the rich leaf mold with a stick, he discovered flat stones laid in a pavement. A paved path ought to lead to something special. This path between the trees, however, led to nothing but a jungle of vines growing over a low mound, a sapling or two striving to thrust up the upper air, and a clump of the loveliest gold-flecked lily bells he'd ever laid eyes on.

He had to have a root of that lily for his garden. Up the mound he scrambled, tearing at vines, butting his way through dense greenery. A little way more and he'd be able to reach out his hand and touch the stems.

Jan didn't get any nearer. With a soft sushssing sound the earth gave beneath him, and he would have fallen into a hole if he hadn't quickly rolled to one side and hung on for dear life to a prickly-leafed bush.

"*Hej*, that was a close one." Catching breath, and assuring himself that he was still all in one piece, the boy peered cautiously into the opening gaping beside him.

"No, no," he murmured, staring at a framework of wooden timbers, at the piece of rotted wood that had broken beneath his weight. "No, it can't be."

But it was. The mound was really a little house that years and years ago had sunk part way into the bog and been covered up by earth and vines, and he had broken through the roof. The hole led down into a dark, musty-smelling place.

Jan was hunching his shoulders forward over the opening, straining his eyes to see what could be inside the long-buried house. But a hoarse sound, "Baw-ump, Baw-ump," suddenly rolled out and sent him sliding down the mound at a great rate, as he remembered Philip's tales of ancient ghosts in the swamp depths.

Back on the raft and poling homeward, Jan told himself that he didn't believe in ghosts, of course. That old bellowing thing was likely

enough a bullfrog. Anyway, he wasn't interested in things underground. Plenty of wonderful things on top of the earth to keep him busy.

But the mystery of the buried house refused to be shut out of Jan's mind. He wanted to keep it secret, yet he also longed to show it to someone.

Finally, with a treat of candy bars in his pocket, he invited Tilka for a ride on the raft down Big Creek.

While Jan poled, Tilka sat cross-legged on the boards, nibbling chocolate, her eyes noting flashes of bird wings, seeking out flowers along the way. "Look, look!" She was pointing to a fragrant pink orchid with bearded lip.

As they followed the twistings of the creek deeper into the swamp, she fell silent. Uneasiness seemed to well up inside her. "Jan," she whispered, "let's turn back now."

"Not yet." The boy was suddenly stubborn. "We're almost there. I've got something to show you."

With the expertness of much doing, Jan brought the raft to his island, moored it to the willows, and helped his passenger ashore.

"Follow me." He led off around the edge of the island, and Tilka obediently trailed after. Like a guide conducting a tour, he showed her the old posts sunk in the bog, making sort of a stepping-stone bridge across to the smaller island. He led her cautiously up the mound to peer into the roof hole.

"That is something to see, no?" he exclaimed triumphantly. "A lost house, and nobody knows where it is but you and me."

Tilka stared soberly into the black hole. "A house nobody knows about—a safe place to hide," she muttered.

"You and your hiding, bah!" Jan turned away angrily. "We've come to a safe land. No need to be scary and always hunting a place to hide."

A tear spilled down Tilka's cheek. Snatching up a piece of vine, she began fumblingly to loop it into the linked circles of the Sign. "Re-remember this." She sobbed, holding it up. "My life it saved—and yours too—when we had to hide. I never forget the Sign. Always it helped us find each other in the terror-time."

Suddenly gentle, Jan patted her shoulder. "Now, now, don't cry. All that bad time is past."

"Yah—yes." With an effort Tilka managed a watery smile. "Like you say, all is good now."

They rode home in silence. But when he moored the raft at the land ridge, Jan said, "Mind you, not a word to anyone about the lost house."

"I promise." Tilka nodded soberly.

As they entered the kitchen they found the rest of the family in happy excitement. Letters had come from abroad, letters from kin and friends in the refugee camp, thanking them for the packages of food. For Papa and Mama letters from Cousin Anton and Cousin Irena. Also a letter addressed to Jan, a pencil scrawl on a bit of wrapping paper —from Rodyn, the old woodcarver, thanking him for the gift of food, and ending with the message, "Do not forget, little friend. The time draws near."

"What does he mean?" asked Mama. "What are you not to forget?"

"Oh, just some stuff he told me." And Jan slipped out of the room before she could question him further.

For a week Jan marked off days on the calendar hanging on the kitchen wall. Then, after one of those spring nights when the moon seemed to shine right on into the dawn, the boy went down to the swamp in the dim early morn. After getting the tin box with the wooden locket out of its hollow-tree hiding place, he loosed the raft from its mooring and poled down the creek to his island.

There the boy knelt and made a little ritual of scraping something off the locket's carving and burying the scrapings in a trench in the ground, mumbling under his breath:

"When the moon rides high,
  In the daylight sky,
  With a pledged secret hand,
  Share the old's riches
  With a new land."

Tenderly his fingers smoothed the ground over the trench. Then Jan put the wooden locket into the tin box, shut the lid tight, and thrust it into a new hiding place under a cypress log.

"No need to be scary!" Jan had told Tilka that, and Tilka tried to forget her fears. But one day there was a loud blast and a huge column of smoke rose in the road. That was how the terrible war guns had sounded! And Tilka and little Betsy Foster were all alone. Tilka forgot she was in safe America. She snatched up Betsy and ran! When Jan came home, Tilka and Betsy were gone, and some people were saying Tilka had kidnaped the little girl. Jan knew he must find Tilka quickly. But where was she hiding? He had only one hope. Perhaps Tilka would remember the Sign that had helped them find each other in the terror time.

Fear clutched Jan and sent him on a second tearing search across the island—through the willow thickets and the clumped palmettos, then right back again to the sunken house.

Here was where they must be. Here was where Tilka had said was the good place to hide. He wriggled again through the jagged opening in the earth-covered roof, slid down the knotted rope. His flashlight pointed faint beams beneath the crude table, behind the high-backed bench. It wavered on over the fallen mound of chimney clay, over the heavy old door jammed so solidly shut.

178   Then—ek! He was in darkness!

Jan shook the electric torch, frantically thumbed the metal slide, but no light came on. Battery gone dead, that was what!

It was dark night out there in the upper world, and a deeper, darker night down here in this moldy closed-in space. The boy stood rigid, listening. There, in that corner, something slithery moved. Night in an underground house was no place for him. He clawed for the hanging rope, hauled himself up the slant of the wall and into the open air again.

Night had trapped him on the island. He couldn't leave now—not on that flimsy raft that might crack to pieces under him.

Nobody knew where he was. He hadn't helped things. And what a mess he'd rushed himself into!

He bumped from tree to tree, finally reached the towering beech, and climbed up until he could settle in a spreading crotch, his back to the trunk, and a vine knotted across his body to steady him. It was better here, above creeping, crawling ground things. He tried to drag his thoughts together. What was happening back on the mainland? Had Mrs. Trotter stirred up her hunt? What would Mamma and Papa think when they got back to—to everybody upheaved and stirred-up against them?

What to do next? Jan pressed a hand against his head, as if to press ideas out of it. But he was so tired. For a whole eternity he had been running and tugging and struggling. Leaden weights seemed to thrust him down, down. He sagged against the tree.

Sleep claimed him. Then he woke with a start, snatching at something that was cutting into his stomach—just the vine about his middle to remind him that he had tied himself up in a tree crotch.

He dozed again, woke again—a restless night. Things bellowed in the distance, things slipped and slished in the bushes beneath him. A cold touch on his hand—was it a snake, or just twigs moving? Away, away off he heard dogs barking. Once he glimpsed faint flashes of light. He yelled mightily but got no reply.

He shivered in the swamp dampness, huddled close to the tree trunk.

The boy woke with a start. Pale light was pinking the sky. Jan slid stiffly down from his tree perch. Now that he could see, he knew 179 what he must do. There was still one place to look. He went to it on reluctant feet, crossing the island to the side bound by the sucking bog that was set with stepping-posts. In the dawn-light he moved slowly along the shore. A footprint showed in crusty mud—several prints. And—yes, here lay two circles of withered swamp grass, knotted into the Sign. Tilka had made that. Tilka had come this far. Had she got across the bog?

He let out a yell—more yells. No answer.

He was turning off, then whirled back and began to whistle the fluting lilt of a Polish folk-song. A fluting whistle answered him.

There was movement in a thicket. Tilka eased out, stood on the shore, facing him across the bog.

"Oh, Jan! I knew you'd come." She stood there, crying and talking, her words running together. "So frightened—the boom-boom, like the great guns. All of a sudden it seemed they'd be after us again—for the camp. I—I had to hide. And that woman, screaming and running —she *left* little Betsy. I had to save her too."

"Tilka, Tilka!" Jan kept calling to her. "Don't be frightened any more. You are safe—safe! That booming was just workmen blasting big rocks, getting the road made."

Tilka nodded but kept on crying, her hand on her scar.

"Folk will understand," soothed the boy. "They'll know you did the best you could. I think you are a h-heroine for trying to save Josef and Betsy when you were so scared yourself. Are they all right?"

"Me all right," piped a voice. A pink frock popped through the thicket, and the little girl hugged Tilka's knees.

"Me too," said Josef and eased out into the open.

"Tilka carried Betsy over first," piped the little girl proudly.

"Josef waited, good as gold," broke in the small boy. "Tilka came back for Josef and for Binkie. Binkie, he followed, couldn't be left behind." And, at that a yellow puff of fur came bounding out of the leaves.

"Heavens!" Jan simply roared it across the bog. "You, Tilka—how did you carry everything?"

"I was so s-scared," said Tilka. "Reckon I was strong as S-Samson."

"It was fun," said Betsy. "Like camping out. The quilt made a nice tent—only it smelled of sulphur—ooey-fooey!"

"Ek! you thought of lime-sulphur!" squawked Jan.

"Against snakes." Tilka nodded. "Dropped some in my pocket. Didn't know how long we'd be here."

Jan looked down at the bog, the slimy mass set with ancient stepping posts. He looked up. Tilka had been staring at the bog too. He caught her eye, held it, said slowly and firmly, "You had best wait where you are, Tilka. You promise me?"

The girl nodded.

"Cross your heart?"

She nodded again, hands solemnly making the cross upon her breast.

"I'll go as fast as I can. I'll bring back the big rope. We'll fix a sort of bridge—that'll be safer for all of you to cross by."

Jan turned away, turned back. "The raft, our good raft! Where—?"

Tilka told him where she had hidden it, and Jan hurried to the other side of the island. As he parted a thick screen of vines and found the raft tied to a tree in a sheltered cove, he thought admiringly, "That Tilka, a real swamper! Knew how to get in here." He had other thoughts, not so pleasant. Tilka, running off with a neighbor's child, trying to save Betsy along with herself! Poor Tilka, she meant so well, but would folk understand? How was this affair going to turn out? He shivered. Would the community turn against the Voda family, kick them out? Jan fell to poling too hard to let himself think.

So much had happened in so short a time. The sky was still streaked in the pink and gray of early dawn when Jan bumped the raft to the ridge-end, knotted the tie-rope to its stake, and hurried toward home. Halfway out of the swamp he glimpsed Bill Trotter, but Bill turned and ran at the sight of him.

At the swamp-edge Jan was met by a surging group of angry people fetched by Bill—people weary and mud-streaked, some carrying poles and guns, some still swinging lighted lanterns that flickered smokily in the dawn. Hands clamped down on Jan's shoulders. Voices shouted things at him. "Betsy Foster—where is she? Kidnaper! Dirty foreigner!"

Words, words—they surged around him! Terrifying words! He couldn't understand half of them. In his anguish, all the American 181 words Jan knew seemed to fly out of his brain. He stammered and stuttered in Polish and made motions with his hands.

Other people rushed into the group—Mamma and Papa. Oh, heaven be praised! Mr. Foster—a man with him that somehow looked familiar to Jan. (Where could he have seen him? Too much worry to bother with that now.) Still others came—Mrs. Trotter, shouting and pointing; Mrs. Foster, trembling with the horror of last night's late return, her baby gone, search parties looking in wells, combing woods and roads.

Philip shouldered in, muddy and haggard. At Jan's despairing gesture, Philip came over to stand beside him. Jan's words poured out. Polish, nothing but Polish could he think in. The other boy shook his head, stooped, grabbed a little stick, thrust it into Jan's hand, pointed to the ground.

Picture-talk—that was what Philip meant! Oh, blessed relief of a way to get thought relayed to another human being! Jan knelt, holding the stick tightly, concentrated a moment. Then, in a clear space on the ground, he drew a great wavering circle, laid a finger on it, motioned toward the swamp.

Philip nodded his head.

On went Jan's stick, drawing a crude map of the swampland—the twisting, winding line of Big Creek, a circle for one island, another circle close by for the second island, and, upon this, a quick sketch of three figures, one of them tall, two of them small. And now, with the tension going out of him, words began to come back to Jan. "Good," he said. No, that wasn't the word—ai, he had it. "Safe, safe, safe!" He shouted it over and over.

With Philip helping him, Jan finally made it known that the lost children must be rescued from across a bog. Cords, ropes, maybe a box or a chair would be needed.

In that awful first moment of their return to an empty house last night, the Vodas had seen the inky mark of the linked circles dabbed on the kitchen floor; had read its meaning of flight. With the swamp so near, the man had started work on the raft he knew would be needed. Now this was dragged down and launched.

With horn tooting, a car came bumping across the pasture, and

roped atop it was the boat that had been telephoned for. This, with the two rafts, bore the Fosters, the Vodas, and a few others down slow-moving Big Creek toward Jan's island. Back on shore, somebody fired three pistol shots, the agreed signal to tell other searchers that the lost ones had been located.

Nobody talked much. The women sat in a little huddle. Men and boys bent their strength to rowing and poling the three crafts through the eerie dimness of the swamplands.

At the Island of the Hidden House, Jan landed first and led on across to the bog side. He stood for a moment, shouting and waving at the girl and her two little charges on the other shore. He looked down at the bog and shivered. But if Tilka had crossed it, so could he.

He turned for a quick whispered word with Philip. After thrusting a ball of cord into his friend's hand, with directions to keep it unwinding, Jan ran swiftly out over the quaking bog, setting feet on those buried posts, whose tops he could just see. Suppose he made a misstep? Suppose—but Tilka had done it; so could he. There, he was across!

A shout went up behind him.

Now everything would be easy. The cord that spanned the bog was the first link in the bridge across danger. A light rope was tied to the cord's end, and Jan began to draw that over. Attached to this was the great rope that had a box and a pair of pulleys hung on to it. Jan and Tilka, tugging mightily, finally got an end knotted about a stump. Across the way, men tied the other end of the hawser to a tree trunk, as high up as they could reach. Ek-a, good! That lifted the ropeway and its sliding seat above the muck.

Settled safely in the box, first little Betsy was drawn across; then Josef, all a-grin with the fine adventure, and holding tight to yellow Binkie. After them came Jan and Tilka, crossing on the posts, but with the rope handy as a safety rail.

Parents clutched their little ones in their arms. Jan stood to one side, patting Tilka, who had burst into weeping, moaning about bombs and foolish fright. The Voda family drew together, uneasy, expecting to be harshly used because one of them had made such a foolish mistake as to think road-blasting was enemy bomb-explosions.

But instead, here came Mr. Foster, thrusting out a hand to grip

Mr. Voda's hand. And here was Mrs. Foster, drawing Tilka to her in a warm hug and saying, "No, no, we couldn't be angry with 'mine Tilka,'" when she was trying to protect our Betsy."

Philip drew Jan off to whisper to him that the one his folks really blamed was that Mrs. Trotter, for rushing off and leaving Betsy scared and crying, alone in the house.

And Mrs. Trotter, who had got to the island on the second raft-load, kept on mumbling that she had just yelled to the foreigner to shut her windows to keep out the explosion dust—that she just *had* to go shut her own windows to keep out that awful dust.

Safe! Safe! Everyone was safe. The new life for the Voda family was safe. What a wonderful feeling!

All happy and relaxed, Jan sidled up to the tall man standing near Mrs. Foster, motioned him to one side. "You were here. You fell into the hidden house and sprained the ankle."

The tall man nodded.

"But why," Jan went on, "did you say, 'Tell no one you saw me'?"

The tall man grinned. "Because I'm her brother Bob." He nodded at Mrs. Foster. "She'd have been mad if I got this close and passed up a visit. But I had come to get some of this." His hand touched a plant with stiff red leaves. "It is a very rare plant."

"I know—yes," said Jan eagerly, "about it, I read in the bo-tan-i-cal book—supposed to grow only one place in the world, in that Georgia swamp. But we see it here. The Old One who built the house that sunk, maybe he made it to grow here, as he did other so strange plants. See—some of them I have tended and brought back to blooming."

The man knelt, gently touching finger to a small low-growing plant with quaint pink blossoms, and next bent above a spotted-leafed shrub with queer green bells. Then he murmured, "You have tended plants so rare they are almost lost to the rest of the world."

He got to his feet, walked a few steps. "And do I see—do I really see this?" He stood gazing at a row of tall straight stalks, each branching out at the top into a crown of bright blue flowers. He murmured softly, "The fabulous *Polessia Linacae.* Am I seeing a little bit of Poland, the royal flax?"

"Yes, yes," said Jan, all smiles. "You see it—my secret, my hidden   185 thing in the swamp."

"But how—where—"

"Wait, I show you." Jan was off on a run, came sprinting back, carrying a tin box. Out of it he took the wooden locket. He opened it, laid it in Mr. Bob's hand. "Look hard, you can see them—just a few of the so tiny flax seed still left here, glued to the wood, looking like little bumps in the carving. I scraped off and planted the rest of the seed, just as old Rodyn told me to. He gave me the locket as a parting gift, whispered to me the secret that Poles could only be happy in a land where a little bit of Poland grew. The famous seed—he brought them out of my own land when he himself escaped." The boy's voice dropped. "Polish flax now blooms in America. Will Poles find happiness here?"

"Polish folk," said Mr. Bob, "can make their happiness here, as you are making yours. You—you will grow into a very great botanist some day—maybe the greatest of them all."

A Penny's Worth of Character

BY JESSE STUART

Illustrated by Robert G. Henneberger

This is the story of Shan, a country boy who did not often have money to spend on the things he liked best. One day Shan found a way to get nine pennies. But he needed ten cents for his favorite treat, a lemon soda pop and a chocolate candy bar. Shan wondered where he could get the extra penny—until he suddenly decided he wouldn't need it! He would trick Mr. Conley, the storekeeper, into giving him the pop and candy bar for one cent less than it cost. What did that one penny matter? Shan found out that it mattered a lot, and so will you as you read his story.

"SHAN, I WANT YOU TO GO to the store for me this morning," his mother said. "I've got a list made out of things I need."

Shan's mother, Millie Shelton, was doing the family wash before the sun got high enough to shine down into the deep green valley. When the sun got high, the day grew warmer and the flowers wilted on their stems. Then it was almost too hot to rub clothes on a washboard over a tub of warm soapy water.

"Mom, you got some eggs for me to take to Mr. Conley?" Shan asked.

"Not this morning," she replied. "Our hens aren't laying too well this time of year. We're not getting more eggs than we need for ourselves."

Shan was disappointed. When Shan carried eggs to the store, there were always a few pennies left over after he'd traded the eggs for groceries. His mother let him have these extra pennies to buy candy. Shan was always happy if there were as many as three pennies left over. He bought peppermint sticks and gumdrops with these. Sometimes there was a whole nickel left over and then he bought

187

his favorite chocolate bar. And sometimes—rarely—there was a dime left to buy the chocolate bar and a lemon soda pop, too. He ate the chocolate bar and drank his lemon soda pop at the same time. The two were so good together that when he thought about them he got hungry. He had never tasted anything better in his life than a chocolate bar when he had a cool lemon soda pop to wash it down.

His mother noticed his disappointment. "Shan, there is a pile of empty sacks in the smokehouse," his mother said. "You can trade them for candy. Don't take the one over on the right by itself—it has a hole in the bottom of it. I'll probably be able to use that one for peaches."

"Thanks, Mom. I'll get them."

He began to smile as he thought of the candy he would get at Mr. Conley's store.

Shan ran to the smokehouse and opened the door. He hurried in and found the sacks stacked up neatly on a chair. There were more than he expected. He counted one, two, three, four, five, six, seven, eight—and very slowly he counted the ninth sack. He had hoped there would be ten. Ten large sacks equaled a dime. And with a dime he could get his favorite chocolate bar and lemon soda pop.

Shan stood there thinking. Then he went over and looked at the tenth sack with a hole in it. It sure was too bad this sack had a hole in it.

He tiptoed to the smokehouse door and looked out to see where his mother was. She was walking across the yard with another basket heaped high with clothes. She was taking them to the clothesline. The clothesline was on the other side of the yard from the smokehouse. He waited until she set the basket down and started pinning up the clothes. Then he put the nine sacks under his arm and started out.

He stopped; then he went back. He picked up the tenth and looked at the hole. "Not really much of a hole," he said to himself. "A pretty useful old sack if you didn't put stuff like sugar or meal into it."

He knew how Mr. Conley took the top sacks from the pile and held them up to the lighted window and looked inside to see if any light came through. But Mr. Conley was old and he might not be seeing too well. And besides, Mr. Conley never looked at all the sacks. He

might look at some on the top and some on the bottom of the pile, but he wouldn't hold every one in the pile up to the light.

Suddenly Shan knew the way to fool Mr. Conley. He put a good sack down. This was number ten. Then he laid down number nine and eight. These were good sacks too. Then he put the sack with a hole in it down for number seven. He placed six good sacks on top. This would throw Mr. Conley off either way he looked. If he looked at the sacks from the top or the bottom, it wouldn't matter now.

Shan smiled as he picked up the paper sacks and held them under his arm. His troubles were over. He had found the way to get what he wanted. He could have both the chocolate bar and the lemon soda, and shucks, what did one little old hole amount to? He walked through the door and stepped onto the soft green grass.

Mr. Conley's store stood where The Valley joined the Sandy River road. It was a little one-room building, painted white, under a grove of sycamore trees. Shan loved this store, and when he saw it he always broke into a run to get there. He was happy as he had ever been on this August morning when he stepped up the three little steps into the store.

"Good morning, Mr. Conley," he said.

"Good morning, Shan," Mr. Conley greeted him.

Mr. Conley was standing behind the candy counter. Shan walked up and peeped through the glass to see if Mr. Conley had his favorite chocolate bars. They were under the glass all right. Shan counted six of them. He wished he had enough sacks to trade for all six.

"Gee, Mr. Conley, I was afraid you wouldn't have the chocolate bars," Shan said.

"Yes, Shan, those bars are mighty popular," he said. He walked from behind the counter.

Mr. Conley was a little man. He was bent with age.

"Have you brought me some sacks this morning, Shan?" he asked.

"Yes, I have," Shan replied.

"I'm glad you've brought them," he told Shan. "I need them now. I'm nearly out of large paper sacks. Customers buy flour and meal in small lots and I've used all my sacks."

"I'm glad you want 'em, Mr. Conley," Shan said.

But Shan's heart pounded a little faster when Mr. Conley took the sacks from under Shan's arm.

"Got any holes in 'em?" Mr. Conley asked.

"You . . . y-y-y'd better see for yourself, Mr. Conley," Shan stuttered.

"I always examine them to see if there are any holes," Mr. Conley said.

Shan felt the blood rush to his face. And his heart pounded faster than it did when he was running down The Valley. Mr. Conley laid the paper sacks upon the counter. He took the first one and held it toward the window. He opened the sack and looked inside.

"That sack's all right," Mr. Conley said. "When I hold one up against the light in the window and look in, if there's a hole big as a pin-point it will show big as a dime."

Shan didn't say anything. He couldn't think of anything to say. Even if he could have thought of anything, he couldn't have said it. His tongue felt as if it had been tied down with a twine string— the kind Mr. Conley used to wrap packages. Shan stood there silently as Mr. Conley lifted up sacks two, three, four, and looked in.

"These are all right, Shan," he said. "I've not found a hole big as a pinpoint."

Then Mr. Conley picked up sack number five.

Surely he won't look at any more, Shan thought.

"This one is all right," Mr. Conley said as he laid it over with the other good ones.

Shan stood there hoping he wouldn't pick up another sack. But he watched Mr. Conley's small nervous white hand as it went down to pick up the sixth sack. Shan felt a warmer glow come over his face. And his heart pounded faster than ever while he watched Mr. Conley open the sack and look in.

"This one's all right," he said and put that sack with the other good ones.

When Mr. Conley reached for the seventh sack, a box of cereal fell from the shelf.

"What was that?" Mr. Conley asked, turning to Shan.

"A box fell off the shelf," Shan murmured.

"I thought somebody had come in the store," Mr. Conley said as he turned back to the sacks. "But when a man gets seventy years old his ears are not as good as they have once been. They get like an old paper sack that has been used so many times it's got holes in it!"

Shan looked up from the floor just in time to see Mr. Conley's little nervous hand go down for another sack.

Oh, I hope and pray he doesn't get that seventh sack, thought Shan.

Shan got his breath easier and his heart slowed down a bit when Mr. Conley took the last sack from the bottom. He lifted it up and looked in.

Sweat ran in little streams down Shan's face now. Mr. Conley reached down and picked up sack number nine. There were only two sacks left. He held number nine and looked at it in a hurry. His hand went down again and rested on the eighth sack. That just left the sack with the hole in it.

"Shan, how many sacks did you bring?" he asked, turning around slowly and looking at Shan.

"T-t-ten, Mr. C-C-Conley," Shan stammered.

Mr. Conley counted slowly. "One, two, three, four, five." This was one pile. "Six, seven, eight, nine, ten."

Shan felt a great relief. Then Mr. Conley picked up the second pile 191 and placed it on top of the first one. Shan knew that meant Mr. Conley would have just one good sack to use before he came to the bad one.

"I'll bet I know what you want for these sacks." Mr. Conley teased Shan as he walked toward the candy case. "You want chocolate bars."

"One chocolate bar, Mr. Conley," he said. "And I want a lemon soda pop."

"All right, my boy," Mr. Conley said, taking slow steps to the candy case. "You'll have the lemon soda pop and the chocolate bar."

Shan's hand was still sticky where he had wiped his face. And when Mr. Conley gave him the chocolate bar, it stuck to his hand. Then Mr. Conley took a cold lemon soda pop from the icebox. He opened the bottle and gave it to Shan. The ice-cold bottle felt good in his hot hand.

"Did your mother send for anything, Shan?" Mr. Conley asked. "I see you fetched a basket."

"Yes, sir," he replied. "The list is in the bottom of the basket."

Shan turned the bottle up to his mouth. He was in a big hurry to taste again his favorite drink. He swallowed and tasted and then he looked at the bottle. It was lemon soda pop but it didn't taste like the others he'd got at Mr. Conley's. It wasn't as good as the others had been. Then he took a bite from his chocolate bar. It had a funny taste too. It didn't taste as good as the other chocolate bars Mr. Conley had sold him. He looked at the wrapper; it was the same kind of chocolate bar he had been getting. He looked around to see where Mr. Conley was. He was reading the list Shan's mother had sent.

Shan took another bite from the chocolate bar. Then he followed it with a cool drink of his soda pop. That's the way he had always done. He'd eaten one and drunk the other and the two were wonderful together. But they weren't so good now. There was something funny about the taste of both. He took another bite of the chocolate bar and another drink of soda pop. He was in a hurry because Mr. Conley had filled the basket and was fetching it to him. Then Mr. Conley might go back to the sacks. He hurried to finish the chocolate bar and he almost choked. But he washed the bite down with another drink of soda pop.

"I have everything your mother wanted, Shan," Mr. Conley said, setting the basket down on the counter.

Shan hated to leave any lemon soda pop in the bottle. He put the bottle to his lips while Mr. Conley stood there watching him. He couldn't swallow the last drink. He choked and the soda pop almost strangled him. He set the bottle on the counter and grabbed his basket and ran from the store. Mr. Conley stood shaking his head as Shan ran out the door and down the steps. The fresh air outside the store was better for Shan. Still, he didn't feel just right as he began running up The Valley road for home.

"Shan, what happened to that flour sack with a hole in the bottom?" his mother asked as soon as he reached home.

She stood before him and pointed a finger. There was a frown on her face.

"Answer me, Shan," she said, as she took the basket from his hand.

Shan moved his bare feet restlessly over the stone doorstep. He looked down at his feet for he couldn't look up at his mother.

"Did you take that flour sack down to Mr. Conley's store?" she asked him again.

"Yes, Mom," he replied.

"I thought I told you not to take it!"

"You did."

"Then why did you do it?"

"I don't know."

"Did Mr. Conley go over the sacks to see if any had holes in 'em?"

"Yes, he did," Shan said.

"Why didn't he find the hole in that sack?" she then asked him. 193

"He didn't look through all of 'em," Shan said.

"You're lucky," she said. "But didn't you know it was wrong to do this? Didn't you know you were cheating Mr. Conley for a penny?"

"Yes, Mom," he said.

"Then why did you do it?"

"I wanted a dime, Mom," he said. "If I had taken nine sacks, I would have had only nine cents. I wanted a chocolate bar and a bottle of lemon soda pop. That took a dime."

"You know I never taught you to do a thing like this, don't you?" his mother said.

And then she didn't say another word. She turned and walked back through the house with the basket. Shan's thought spun around and around and over and over in his head for he wondered what his mother was going to do now. He didn't have long to wait to find out what it was. She came back immediately with a new sack.

"Let this be a lesson to you," his mother said. "Take this sack to Mr. Conley to replace the no-good one. Tell him just what has happened."

"Oh no, Mom," he said, "I . . . I . . . can't. . . ."

"You *will*," she said firmly.

"Won't you just whip me and let me stay here?" he begged, beginning to cry. "I don't want to tell Mr. Conley what I've done."

"Go back and make things right," his mother said. "You will think before you ever do this again."

Shan looked up at his mother and his eyes were filled with tears.

"I want to say one more thing, Mom," he said. "It's just one sack that's only worth a penny."

"One penny or a hundred pennies, Shan, the principle is the same," his mother told him. "Do you remember that story your teacher told you about Abraham Lincoln when he was working in the store? He made a mistake of just a couple of pennies when he was giving a woman her change. Abraham Lincoln walked miles after a hard day's work to return it to her. That's how important it was to him. It made him feel better inside. Make you feel better too."

Shan stood before his own front door crying. He didn't want to

go back.

"Dry your tears," his mother told him. "Be on your way!"

There wasn't anything for Shan to do but turn and go back to the store, carrying one little light paper sack. The sack was only worth a penny and he had a mile to walk there and back. As he walked down the road with the sack under his arm, he turned and looked back to see what his mother was doing. She was standing at their front door watching him walk slowly under the August sunlight down the hot, dusty road.

Earlier in the morning, when Shan had gone to the store with his ten sacks, the world had belonged to him. But now it was different. He walked under a hot sun down the dusty road and this world didn't belong to him. This was a world he didn't want. When he reached the giant sycamore where he had watched the big red-headed woodpecker early that morning boring for worms, he stopped long enough to look up to see if the bird was back again, for it would soon be time for lunch. But the woodpecker had gone and the dead limb looked hot and dry in the August sunlight. He wondered where the woodpecker had gone and if he was in a cool nest in some hollow tree with his family of young birds away from the hot sun.

Beyond the sycamore, he walked over sand that was hot to his feet. The buttercups, over which the honeybees and bumblebees were humming two hours ago, were dry and wilting in the heat.

When Shan reached the big white oak, he wondered if bees and birds sweated as he did. He thought the birds didn't, for when the sun got hot, he never saw many birds—they were always in the cool shade. They gathered food in the morning when it was cool. He looked over the steep bank by the white oak at the deep water hole. The minnows weren't swimming around either. He saw them resting down there in the shaded water. A lazy minnow swam up, expecting Shan to throw a cracker crumb or a green fly, but Shan didn't—he didn't have time. And the minnow wasn't as pretty as it had been that morning when Shan felt the world belonged to him. He'd let the minnows find their own food. He had to work to get his. Look what the chocolate bar and the soda pop had cost him! He wasn't through yet. Look what a time he was having. Besides his bare feet were hot from walking over the sun-baked sand.

When he waded into the stream he touched a rock with his foot and a crawdad came out swimming backward. Shan didn't stop to watch it swim. He waded under the willow shades where the water was cooler to his feet. But he was careful not to splash water on the good sack he was carrying. He knew he had to give that to Mr. Conley. And he had to tell him about the sack with the hole in it. He dreaded to do that, too. He hoped there wouldn't be any customers to hear him.

When Shan walked over the sand bar, he didn't stop. He walked on and dried his tears from his eyes the best he could with the back of his hand. The turtle that had come to the sand bar to lay her eggs that morning was somewhere under the cool shade of the alder and the willow beside the stream.

Leaves on the big sugar maple were wilted too. The hawks were no long circling in the high blue sky. Shan walked slowly down the dusty road beyond the maple, thinking about Mr. Conley and the sack. He wondered what he would say when he gave it to him. He didn't want to take this sack to Mr. Conley.

Shan thought of running away from home. He thought about taking to the hills and going in any direction that would take him from home. Then he wondered how he could leave his father. His father didn't have any part in making him take the sack back. And he thought about how hard it would be to stay away from his baby brother and his little sisters. Shan wanted to make his mother feel sorry for sending him back to the store with a sack worth a penny.

But there wasn't anything left for him to do but to face Mr. Conley. To think of returning this sack made his face get hotter than the sun could make it. He tried to think of what he was going to say. But his tongue got heavy again. It was as lazy as the wind and didn't want to speak these words. It would only be a few minutes. He couldn't tell his heart to beat slower and he couldn't keep his face from getting hotter.

He walked around the bend in the road where the cliffs looked up to the hot blue sky. This was the first time in Shan's life he hadn't wanted to see Mr. Conley's little white store under the sycamore trees. Always before, when he had walked around the winding road beneath these cliffs and seen the store, he had started running to get there. He saw two horses, with saddles on, hitched to the sycamore limbs. There was a team of horses hitched to a wagon standing in front of the store. Shan thought, people are in the store and they will hear what I have to tell Mr. Conley. I'll wait until they leave before I give him this sack.

Shan stopped outside and looked in. There were three men inside. Tom Eversole picked up his basket of groceries and walked out. Then Shan walked softly inside and listened to Mr. Conley count the eggs Manuel Greene had brought. He watched Manuel Greene trade his eggs for groceries. He stood in the back of the store so quietly they didn't see him. Then Manuel Greene put his basket of groceries on his arm and left the store. Only Tom Crum was left. He asked Mr. Conley for a sack of meal and flour. Mr. Conley picked up the sack on top and filled it full of meal from the barrel. He weighed it to see if he had ten pounds. He had eleven pounds and he slowly dipped a pound out, watching his scales to see that it was correct. Shan watched too.

Then Mr. Conley got the second sack. He dipped a scoop of flour from the barrel into the sack. Then he dipped another and another as if he were in a hurry. Shan saw the flour stream through the corner of the sack like water pouring through the holes in a sieve.

"Woops," Mr. Conley shouted as he put the sack down on the floor as quickly as he could to save the flour.

"Tom, did I tear that sack?" Mr. Conley said, looking up at Tom Crum.

"Don't think you did," Tom replied.

"I just bought this sack about three hours ago from Shan Shelton," he said. "He brought me ten sacks and I looked at nearly all of 'em to see if there were any holes."

Shan was standing behind Mr. Conley and Tom Crum and they hadn't seen him yet.

"These are the first sacks I've used today," Mr. Conley said. "See what it has cost me because I didn't look inside the other two sacks."

"You can't trust young'uns nowadays," Tom Crum said. "They're not raised right."

"Nope, I don't guess you can," Mr. Conley said. "But I'd miss 'em   197 if they didn't come in here and trade me sacks, roots, herbs, eggs, and pelts for candy and soda pop. I like to have 'em around."

When Mr. Conley had finished saying these words he looked back and saw Shan with an empty sack in his hand. He looked straight at Shan. Tom Crum turned around to look.

"Want something, Shan?" Mr. Conley said.

"Yes," Shan said.

He walked up, his heart beating faster and the sweat running from his face. He gave Mr. Conley the sack.

"Just one?" Mr. Conley said.

"Yes," Shan said as Mr. Conley opened the sack to look for holes.

"No use to look for a hole," Shan said.

"Oh," he said, then he laughed as he started to open his candy case.

"No candy for that one, Mr. Conley," Shan said.

"Why, what do you mean?" Mr. Conley asked. "Don't you want the penny?"

"I brought it because—" Shan couldn't finish saying what he wanted to tell Mr. Conley. His tongue was heavier than the wilted pods of leaves hanging over the hot road.

"You've got a good mother," Mr. Conley said.

Shan hadn't told Mr. Conley it was his mother who had sent him back with the sack. He wondered how Mr. Conley knew.

He remembered the thoughts he had had about his mother. He remembered thinking of running away from home to make her feel sorry because she had made him bring the good sack to Mr. Conley.

"There'll be a reserved seat in Heaven for your mother," Mr. Conley said as Shan wiped the tears from his eyes with the back of his hand.

"You'll always be thankful when you grow up your mother made you do this, Shan," Tom Crum said as he rubbed his big rough hand over his beardy face. "This is a lesson in honesty you won't forget. It gives you a good foundation from your finger tips to your toes!"

"Mr. Conley, I'll bring you more sacks to pay for the flour you lost." Shan sobbed and turned to leave the store.

"Since you've been so honest, Shan," Mr. Conley said, smiling, "your debt is paid. I didn't lose much flour. And I think more of you than I have ever thought in my life."

Shan ran from the store. Mr. Conley said something to Tom Crum. Shan didn't hear what he said. He didn't want to hear, for it didn't matter now. The warm lazy wind felt so good to his face. The air was as good and fresh to breathe as it had been when the dew was on the buttercups. The lazy wind dried the flow of tears that had come to his eyes in the store. These were tears he had tried to hold back.

Shan felt as light as a June bug in the August wind. He knew now how Abraham Lincoln felt after he had returned the pennies. Something had left him, and he started running up The Valley road for home. The blue sky above him was as beautiful as he had ever seen it. A red bird chirruped lazily from a cluster of pawpaw and its chirruping was more beautiful than its spring song before an April shower. A hawk sailed over in the lazy wind and it was pretty too. Shan didn't fear anything now. His mother had been right when she said he would feel better within. How did she know all these things? He knew now that his mother was smart and good.

I Hear America Singing

BY WALT WHITMAN

Illustrated by Katherine Grace

I hear America singing, the varied carols I hear,
Those of mechanics, each one singing his as it should be,
   blithe and strong,
The carpenter singing his as he measures his plank
   or beam,
The mason singing as he makes ready for work,
   or leaves off work,
The boatman singing what belongs to him in the boat,
   the deckhand singing on the steamboat deck,
The shoemaker singing as he sits on his bench,
   the hatter singing as he stands,
The wood cutter's song, the ploughboy's on his way
   in the morning, or at noon intermission,
   or at sundown,
The delicious singing of the mother,
   or of the young wife at work,
   or of the girl singing or washing.
Each singing what belongs to him or her and to
   none else,
The day what belongs to the day—
   at night the party of young fellows, robust, friendly,
Singing with open mouths their strong melodious songs.